BEING

MARRIED

TO HER

A NOVEL

Anthony K. Robinson

This is a work of fiction. Names, characters, places, and incidents either are the product of the author's imagination or are used fictitiously, and any resemblance to actual persons, living or dead, business establishments, events, or locales is entirely coincidental. The publisher does not have any control over and does not assume any responsibility for author or third party Web sites or their content.

The scanning, uploading, and distribution of this book via the Internet or any other means without the permission of the publisher are illegal and punishable by law. Please purchase only authorized electronic editions, and do not participate in or encourage electronic piracy of copyrighted materials. Your support of the author's rights is appreciated.

Published by Kyle Robinson Publishing.

TABLE OF CONTENTS

Anthony K. Robinson

CREDITS

Kyle Robinson Publishing
P.O. Box 464523
Lawrenceville GA 30042
www.kylerobinsonpublishing.com
www.beingmarriedtoher.com

Front Cover Design: Perdue Vision, LLC
www.perduevision.com

Photographer: Seven Clicks Photography
www.photosbyseven.com

Body paint: Synthe Maria
www.syntheonline.com

Hair: Masterkutta
www.newrootsbarbershop.com

Makeup: Eboni Harding
eebonimua@gmail.com

Wardrobe: Brian Hampton, The Gentrobe
Brian@thegentrobe.com

Website: Nicole Mewhiney
nmewhiney@hotmail.com

Model: Carolyn Gaudet

Editor: Shani Greene-Dowdell
Imperialpublishinghouse17@gmail.com
www.imperialpublishinghouse.com

ACKNOWLEGEMENTS

To my Angels for your tireless, emotional, financial and never-ending support.

My readers for your patience as I created a heartfelt masterpiece for your reading pleasure!

MarieX for listening to me ramble about my new project and within minutes birthing the title, "Being Married to Her."

Lakesha Denise for taking time out of your day, listening to me and leading me in the direction of getting my second baby into the eyes of my readers.

Dr. Tony Burks II for your dedication to revising "He Was My Husband Too" and making it a better representation of me and Kyle Robinson Publishing.

Dr. Derrick Tennial for your creative vision and guidance in helping me bring this long-awaited story to life.

My late grandmother Mary Etta Slaughter for introducing me to our Lord and Savior in my life and allowing Him to order my steps and with faith, patience and perseverance fulfilling my dreams all in his timing and his way.

My late mother, Gradie Mae Robinson, for her unconditional love and hard work. I credit her for the driven man I am today.

My late sister Margaret Ann Goggans for giving me my name. I guess she knew I'd be Highly Praiseworthy.

Thank you all!
Anthony K. Robinson

DEDICATION

With Love, We Remember
Nona Sheree Billups.

Your Presence We Miss,
Your Memory We Treasure,
Loving You Always,
Forgetting You Never.

CHAPTER ONE

IF THIS ISN'T LOVE

~ Flashback March 2009~

"Hey, babe, how was your day?" Will asked.

"It was a pretty long one, but almost over. I'm down to my last client and should be finishing up in an hour. How was yours, and what time will you be heading home?" I asked.

"Actually, I'm on my way home now. Did you want me to pick us up something for dinner?" Will asked.

"Sure, if you don't mind, get enough for three. Isabella will be joining us, so we can all have a conversation," I said, my voice wavering just a bit.

"Nice, it will be great to see her again. Hope she is well," Will said, and I was glad he didn't pick up on my tone. "Does she have any food restrictions?" he asked.

"All is well with her, and she is looking forward to seeing you, too. Isabella, do you have any food restrictions?" I asked my friend who was sitting in my salon chair getting her hair done.

"No; as long as it's food, I can eat it," she replied with a giggle.

"I heard her," Will said, chuckling. "I'll stop by and pick something up and be home shortly."

"Thanks, and I love you. Be safe driving home," I said.

"Love you too, babe. Please call me when you're leaving the salon," Will said.

"Will do. I'm about to rinse out her color and start blow drying her hair. I'll be calling you soon," I said before ending the call.

"Do you think Will is going to be alright with your decision, or should I try to find someone else?" Isabella asked with a worried expression on her face.

"Don't worry, darling. Of course, he will be alright. He will be supportive of me helping you, knowing it's for a great cause," I tried my best to squelch her worries.

"I take you at your word, and I can't thank you enough," she said, smiling.

I spun her chair around so that she was staring into the mirror.

"OH MY GOD, my hair is beautiful!!" Isabella yelled out.

"Glad you love it. Let me finish sweeping your hair off the floor and cleaning up. Wait in the sitting area, and I'll be up shortly."

After I finished cleaning up, I grabbed my cell phone and dialed Will's number.

"Hello," Will answered.

"Hey, we are leaving the salon. See you in about ten minutes," I said.

"I'll start warming the food and setting the table, so we can eat when you all arrive. Be safe, babe," Will said.

"Thanks, see you soon." I hung up, and Isabella and I left the salon.

⚹ ⚹ ⚹

"Is that my beautiful Isabella I smell coming through my door?" Will asked as we entered through the garage.

"Ola' companheiro bonito," Isabella greeted Will with a hello and air kisses.

"Hello, my beautiful princess," Will said extending his arms to her for a hug.

"And how's my handsome, hardworking man?" Will asked, leaning in to kiss me.

"Tired. Let me wash my hands and change clothes right quick. Then, I'll be back down," I said, heading toward the bedroom.

"Will, I'm going to use your powder room if that's okay?" Isabella asked.

"You know where it is. I'll start putting the food on the table so we can eat when Tyler comes back," Will said.

"Sounds great," Isabella said, and then I heard the bathroom door close behind her.

"Babe, where are my favorite gray sweats?" I yelled to Will from the loft off from the owner's suite upstairs.

"I hung them next to your robe behind the bathroom door," Will answered from the kitchen.

"Okay, I see them. Let me slide them on and a tank, then I'll be down in a few," I responded from the bedroom as I placed my cell on the nightstand to charge.

"The food smells so delicious, Will. Thanks for picking it up for us," Isabella said.

"You're welcome. I hate we don't get to see one another as much," Will said to her with a friendly smile.

"Okay, I'm back guys. Can I help with anything?" I asked as I walked into the kitchen.

"Not at all. You and Isabella take a seat. I've placed the food and beverages on the table already," he beamed. "Babe, you can bless the food," Will said to me after we were all seated at the table.

"I will if you guys don't mind. I have a lot to be thankful for," Isabella interjected.

"Fine with me," I said, and Will nodded his approval while reaching for my hand.

"Pai celestial, obrigado por esta comida que estamos prestes a comer, obrigado pela amizade e abenecoe a uniao de Tyler e Will, Amen," Isabella prayed. It was endearing to hear her thank our Heavenly Father for the food we were about to eat and our friendship, but most endearing for her ask God to bless me and Will's union.

"Amen," Will and I said in unison.

"Isabella, would you like a cocktail tonight or will tea suffice?" Will asked.

"Sure, make me one of your fancy drinks, sir," she requested with a burst of laughter.

"I'll just have some water. I'll get it while you make you all's drinks. Isabella, go ahead and fix your plate," I insisted.

"Two drinks coming right up!" Will said and, a few minutes later, he placed the drinks on the table.

"Pass me the chicken please, Isabella," I asked.

"So, babe, I'm curious to know what it is you and Isabella want to speak with me about?" Will pressed.

"I will ask him if you'd like for me to, Tyler," Isabella suggested.

"Thanks love, but I can do it," I assured her.

"I'm listening." Will grew more curious.

"Isabella's grandmother is celebrating one hundred years of life in a couple of months, but her health isn't the best. Her brother told her that her grandmother would love to see her granddaughter marry before she leaves this world." I paused to give Will time enough to soak in what I'd just said.

"Okay…" Will prodded me to continue.

"Being that Isabella is going back to Portugal for her grandmother's birthday, she was hoping I would go with her and marry her while we're there, so she can show her grandmother that she has found a man to love and take care of her."

Will sat back in his seat for an earthshattering moment of silence. I didn't know what was going through his mind as he stared at me. Then, finally, he broke the silence.

"Guess I can only say I support you since you decided to go along with me marrying Robin so I could stay off base, and she could get the medical benefits, right?" Will asked with thoughtful eyes that pried into my soul for understanding.

Though Will had made the connection between my favor to Isabella to that of his marriage to Robin, I sensed a bit of an undercurrent brewing in his aura.

"Who is Robin?" Isabella cut in with a look of complete shock covering her honey golden features.

"It's a long story, too complicated to get you involved, Isabella," I said with a chuckle that I hoped would cut through the tension around the table.

"Tyler is right, Isabella. It's something I did on paper only to help me and Tyler's situation while being beneficial to one of his friends."

"So, babe, back to the matter at hand. How do you feel about me doing this for her?" I asked, wanting to make sure the air was clear between Will and me. He was and would always be my first priority.

"Tyler, I love you very much. I really want us to be the best for each other and that any problems or issues we may have can be communicated and worked through. Know that I do want to marry you one day soon and work on growing our family. If you marrying Isabella is something you need to do to help a friend, then do it. Just know when we both divorce them I want us to marry one another. Marrying you is the answer to my dreams," he answered, squeezing my hand tightly into his.

"Aww, that's so beautiful, Will. I could only dream of having someone love me as much one day. Thank you so much for doing this for me. Would you mind coming to Portugal with us as Tyler's best man?" Isabella asked.

"I would love to, Isabella. Babe, when are you all planning on doing this?" Will asked.

"Her birthday is in July," I said.

"Well, looks like we are going to Portugal in July! Great place to celebrate my birthday month." Will burst into roaring laughter giving Isabella a high five. "And even greater to be able to put a smile on your grandmother's face," Will acknowledged.

"This is going to make her so happy. I will start making the reservations when I get home tonight and have my brother start with the ceremony planning and prepare the guest house for our arrival," Isabella explained.

"I will block my calendar off right now," I said reaching for my mobile.

"Well, you know I always take the month of July off for my birthday anyway, so I'm good," said Will.

"Will, are you going to be fine with Tyler and me sleeping in the bed together while you sleep in the other room to make it look official to my family on the night we wed?" Isabella asked.

"Of course not, as long as he can tiptoe into the room with me a while, so we can have our own personal honeymoon, quietly," Will joked.

"Enough you two. Let's finish our meal so Isabella can get home and make her calls to get the ball rolling on our marriage," I said.

Will looked at me with the silent promise that one day we would have our perfect wedding day. I smiled back acknowledging his promise.

"You're right, Tyler. I'm just so excited and grateful to you both; obrigado ambos," Isabella said, bringing our attention back to her. She had thanked Will and me in her native tongue with water-filled eyes.

"Whatever we can do to help," Will said, standing to embrace her with a hug as I joined in.

"Dinner was great, you guys. May I help clean the kitchen?" she asked.

"No, I can tidy it while Tyler walks you to the car. I know you have a drive ahead of you to get home, and we wouldn't want you on the road too late," Will, the forever thoughtful gentleman that I fell in love with, said.

"Alright, babe. I'll be right back once I see her off," I said, kissing Will's cheek.

"Don't make me wait too long, babe," Will said to me before turning to Isabella to give her a long hug. "Isabella, dirija seguramente; beijos." He told her to 'drive safe, kisses.'

"Beijos, Will," Isabella replied 'kisses' to Will as she pulled away from their hug.

"Tyler, thank you so much. I probably won't sleep tonight. I know that you and Will have your own set of rings; maybe we can go look for a matching set for when we go to Portugal for avò's birthday," Isabella suggested as I walked her to her car.

"That's fine. Let me know you've made it home safely, and we can discuss details tomorrow. Glad to be able to help give your grandmother her last wish, vos amo," I said closing her car door after she got into her car.

Isabella rolled down her window and said, "I love you too, Tyler. Thanks again, friend."

"You're welcome." I waved as she drove away then went back inside to join Will. "Do you need any help, babe," I asked as I entered the kitchen to find him wiping down the counter.

"All done in here. Want to watch television or head on to bed?" he asked.

So thoughtful. This is why I love this man.

"Let's head to the bedroom to shower so I can properly thank my man for being so accepting of my nuptials to my future wife," I said, half teasing but mostly serious.

"Come here," Will said as he playfully pulled me into his muscular arms as I stroked his short curly hair.

"Yes, sir," I coyly replied.

"Don't think for a minute you have to thank me for supporting you being the caring, loving, and giving man that you are. I love you, Tyler. We are a team, nine years strong and counting."

"Te amo, Will," I said, planting the longest kiss onto his soft lips that suckled mine into his to begin the duel of passion that belonged to me and Will exclusively.

"Hmmm, about that shower," he moaned, placing my hand inside his lounge pants to feel the extent of his need to connect with me as soon as possible.

I smiled as I stared into his searing eyes.

"Last one upstairs has to make the bed in the morning," I said then took off bounding up the stairs.

"No fair, babe. You got a head start with those giraffe legs," he laughed loudly as he raced behind me.

"I'll scrub your body then dry you off followed by a foot massage before I pleasure you," I offered.

"Deal," he said, licking his lips in approval.

"I'll put us some music on. Who would you like to hear?" I asked.

"Play that new Jennifer Hudson CD I bought you and put track two on repeat," he suggested.

"Oh, I see what you're trying to do, sir." I turned on "If This Isn't Love" and pressed repeat. I walked toward the bathroom.

"I'll start the water. Don't leave me in here too long." Will winked as he dropped his clothes onto the porcelain bathroom floor. He didn't have to worry about me making him wait; I was only a few steps behind him.

"I want to thank you for three more things," I said, stepping into the shower behind Will.

"What's that, babe?" he asked.

"For picking up dinner, cleaning the kitchen, and for this good love you're about to give me."

"You're welcome for all of them, especially number three. It gives me great pleasure." He smiled looking up at me from his five-ten frame.

"So, tell me, babe, how was your day?" I asked while turning around for him to scrub my back with my exfoliator.

"It wasn't too bad. I went to a high school to speak with the senior class about recruitment," he answered, kissing me on the back of my neck as his hands slid down to my lower back.

I turned around and kneeled down in the shower to give his throbbing extension some attention and noticed his feet.

"What else did you do besides get a pedicure?" I asked.

"Nothing gets past you, huh? A coworker and I went to get pedicures today as I know you like for me to keep them manicured for you," he answered.

"Close your eyes and lean back against the wall, but hold onto the banister," I ordered, lifting his right foot to put in my mouth.

"Alright now. You're starting something, baby. Damn, that feels good. You know how to treat Papi, don't you?" Will asked.

"Yes, I do. Now, shut your mouth and give me the left one," I ordered before putting it in my mouth and massaging it with my tongue.

"Ooooo weee, Tyler that feels so fuckin' good, babe. You're making me forget my thoughts. Damn!"

he moaned a sound so sweet that it alone turned me on.

"Well, I'll leave you to your thoughts and wait for you in the bedroom," I whispered as I grabbed his extended groin before stepping out of the shower.

"Wait, so you're going to just leave me here throbbing and leaking like this?" he asked, and I could hear the desire lacing his tone.

"Umph. I'll be waiting for you, babe," I said and began singing along with the music. "If this isn't love… J. Hud couldn't have said it any better." I stepped out of the shower and away from Will.

"I'm going to stay in here a few more minutes, babe. Will you pass me those eucalyptus bath salts, so I can place down in the drain to open my sinuses?" he asked.

"Sure. Let me know when you want me to dry you off. I'll get your pillows ready for your foot massage. Do you want me to use the Sherlon Salon lemongrass and ginger or lavender foot cream?" I asked.

"Surprise me. Your giving me the foot massage is special enough as it's totally unexpected but well received, babe," he said, 'but you've got to take care of this and help me empty this full sac before we crash." Will pointed to his extended member, which looked absolutely mouthwatering.

"Anything for you, sir," I yelled from across the bedroom.

I took the time to slip into something comfortable for bed and light some candles. By the time the last candle was lit, Will had yelled from the shower.

"Your man is ready, baby," he said.

"Ooooo weee, both of you are ready?" I asked, laughing as I checked out his erection standing beyond the towel I used to dry his wet body.

"Yes sir, so let's make this foot massage quick. I know you'll have to satisfy your urges, but don't spend too much time with my feet in your mouth please," Will said.

I laughed as my hands eased down his legs until they found his beautiful feet.

"You know the more you moan and fall asleep snoring from my massage that makes me more hormonal." I smiled, feeling my body come alive for Will.

"I know you have the power to put me to sleep, but tonight I'm staying awake so I can put *you* to sleep," he teased, causing me to bite down on my lip in anticipation.

✶ ✶ ✶

The next day, I awoke, still feeling in bliss from the night before. I showered and dressed, grabbed my cell and went downstairs to grab a bottle of water. *Bobbie.* I remembered I needed to call Bobbie and Lady T, so I dialed Bobbie first.

"Hello," Bobbie answered her mobile on the second ring.

"How are you today? Do you have plans for lunch?" I asked.

"Not really, sounds like you need to talk. Want to go to our spot?" she asked.

"Yes, please and thanks," I said.

"Tyler, you know you'll have to pick me up. There will be nowhere I can park the truck."

"That is fine. Just let me know when."

"I have one more stop, so you can meet me at the parking lot in about thirty minutes," she suggested.

"Alright, I'll head to the parking lot and wait on you to arrive," I said.

"See you shortly," Bobbie said.

Next, I called Lady T.

"What's going on, Tyler?" Lady T answered.

"On my way to meet Bobbie for lunch and wanted to see what your afternoon is like. Can you meet us, so I can tell you both some news at the same time?" I asked.

"I have to take a conference call at two. Are you thinking before then?" Lady T asked.

"Well, I'm about to pick her up. Then, we're heading to Poor Calvin's. Can you meet us there in about twenty minutes since it's pretty close to your job?" I asked.

"Let me finish up this last project. Then, I'll head over and get us a table. Will it be just us three?" she asked.

"Yes, I'm pulling in the parking lot to wait on her. Then, we are on the way," I answered.

"Okay, cool. Love you, and see you shortly," Lady T said.

After ending the call with her, all kinds of things ran through my mind as I sat waiting what seemed like twenty minutes on Bobbie. I thought about Will being married to Robin and now Isabella needing help. Due to my willingness to help a friend, pretty soon I'd be married to her, and that was putting Will and me in a situation that would push us further from wedded bliss. We wanted so badly to be married to one another, but society put so much judgment on same-sex marriages, and in some places wouldn't even recognize them.

"Life sucks!" I yelled to myself as I noticed Bobbie pulling up.

"Hey there, tall and sexy," Bobbie said, opening the car door a few minutes later.

"Hello, my love. Your uniform is really turning me on," I said and giggled as I leaned in to hug her.

"Ha! How's your day been so far; everything good with you?" she asked with a look of concern covering her tender features. Bobbie was a beautiful woman inside out, and I was blessed to have her as my friend.

"You worry about me too much; I'm cool. Lady T is meeting us for lunch. I'll tell you both what's going on then," I assured her.

"Oh Lord, I ain't going to have to beat her ass, am I?" She laughed out loud.

"You know she's feisty, so don't tempt her," I replied.

"There's a car backing out of a space that you can grab," Bobbie pointed out as we pulled up to the restaurant.

"Perfect, good eye. Thanks."

"That looks like Lady T's Range Rover over there in the valet section. She beat us here," Bobbie said.

"It's possible; she was leaving after finishing a project she was working on," I said as we walk towards the restaurant.

"I just hope I don't have to tag her," Bobbie said as she gathered her purse and stepped out of the car.

"Welcome to Poor Calvin's, two?" the host asked once we were inside.

"No, we are actually meeting the young lady over in the left corner," Bobbie said, waving at Lady T.

"Hey, chick, how have you been doing? Are we being civil today or fighting?" Lady T asked Bobbie.

These two. They never wasted any time to get into an argument, I thought.

Bobbie chuckled. "Honey, if I wasn't in this uniform, didn't have to go back to work, and anxiously waiting to see what Tyler has to talk to us about, I'd mop you across the floor, but let's be cordial today."

"That's a good fantasy you're having." Lady T laughed. "Hey, baby," she stood to give me a hug.

"Hello, my sweetness. Thanks for meeting us on such short notice," I said. "I'll let us order our food first before starting my talk with you ladies. I'm sure there will be plenty of questions following," I added without addressing their forever beef.

"Uh oh, it's going to be that kind of talk? You know I only have an hour with you, sir," Bobbie said.

"It's not like that. Look over the menu; here comes the server," I said, hurrying things along.

"Good afternoon, ladies and gentleman. Welcome to Poor Calvin's. Is this your first time visiting us?" the handsome server asked.

"No, we've all been here before," Bobbie and Lady T chimed together.

"Do you need a moment to look over the menu?" the server asked.

"I think we are ready to order. Are we ladies?" I asked.

"Let's start with you ma'am," he said to Bobbie.

"I will have your lobster fried rice with a Sprite, no ice," Bobbie ordered.

"And you, ma'am?" he asked Lady T.

"I will have your crispy beef, and I would like to substitute the jasmine rice for brown rice, please," she said.

"Sir?" he asked me.

"Let me get your fried chicken with lobster, macaroni and cheese, and water, no ice add lime," I ordered.

"Would you like any starters?" he asked.

"Sure, you can put in an order of calamari, please and thanks," I said.

"Sure thing. I will get your drinks and starter coming right up, and your entrees will be out soon. I'm Asher if you should need anything," he said before walking away.

"Alright, Tyler, I've held it in long enough. What do you have to tell us?" Lady T sounded frustrated.

"Girl calm your nerves and let me FaceTime Lashawn to see if she's available. I'd like to tell her as well." I waved Lady T off. She was going to get this tea at my pace, not hers.

"Well, dial her 'cause our time is running out and so is my patience," Bobbie said, and, on this rare occasion, she and Lady T were on the same team.

"Hey uncle-brother," Lashawn answered the video call. Perfect. I was glad to see her bright smile on the other end.

"What's going on, sister-niece? I have Bobbie and Lady T with me. Are you available to chat a moment?" I asked.

"Sure. Hey ladies. What's going on?" Lashawn asked with a concerned face while shaking her head.

"Tsk Tsk, I only have an hour for lunch, sir!" Bobbie snidely remarked.

"Let me prop the phone up so you can hear, and I will tell you all at once." I bolstered the phone against the napkin holder in the center of the table and looked around at my friends.

"Come on, sir. Spit it out!" Lady T yelled with urgency in her voice.

"Well, you all know my friend from Portugal, Isabella?" I began.

"Yes, the beautiful girl that has that accent I love?" Bobbie asked.

"That's her."

"What about her?" Lady T beckoned me to continue.

"After I finished her hair last night, she and I went to my house, sat down and had dinner with Will. We shared with him that she needs me to marry her before her grandmother dies," I blurted out.

"Oh my God. Is she like really ill and about to die soon?" Lady T asked.

"She turns a hundred years old in a couple of months, and since Isabella is going back home for her birthday, she wanted to marry while there so that her grandmother could see her wed as that's one of her last wishes before she leaves this earth," I filled them in.

"Wait a minute, sir. Hold up! We need to sit down and talk about this. Marriage is not something you do like pouring a mimosa. You're aware of that, right?" Lashawn preached as she rolled her eyes to the back of her head.

"Lashawn, don't be so hard on him. Maybe y'all, should talk in a different setting when you two can talk alone," Bobbie suggested.

"I totally agree with you, Bobbie. I'm not being hard on him. I just don't want him to do some messed up shit like Will did with Robin just so she can have his medical benefits," Lashawn argued. "There are deeper consequences to decisions like that, as I have shared with Tyler that mockery of a marriage between Will and Robin will bring them more than they'll bargain for in the end."

"Here's your calamari and drinks. Your food should be out shortly," Asher cut into our discussion placing the food and drinks on the table.

"Thank you," I said to him, welcoming the distraction.

"I'm going to let you all eat and finish your conversation; Lady T and Bobbie air kisses. Sir, will you call me later this evening, please and thanks?" Lashawn hissed as she ended the video call. I could only imagine what that call would be like later that night.

"Tyler, you're not doing this because Will and Robin are married, are you?" Lady T prodded.

"Girl, please. No, I am not. You know that's only on paper, and he's going to be filing for the divorce soon. As he told you when he asked you, he only wanted to do it for a few years. I'll only be married to Isabella until after her grandmother dies. We're both helping out friends," I reasoned.

"Babe, I mean, we support you in whatever you decide you need to do, and I think it's very noble of you to offer such a beautiful gesture to Isabella for the sake of pleasing her grandmother," Bobbie said.

"Yay! The food is here," Lady T said seemingly glad to have the interruption of the waiter placing our food down on the table.

"We haven't even touched the calamari, so let me bless the food so we can eat, and you ladies can get back to work," I said.

"Before you do, I just want to say I echo Bobbie's comment; we support you wholeheartedly. I yearn for the day to see you and Will walk down the aisle. That was so beautiful when he kneeled before you and proposed to you in front of your mother and all of us on the cruise last year." Lady T raised her glass. "To more beautiful moments like that in the future."

"Thanks, T. Let's pray so we can eat and you ladies can get back to work."

Everyone bowed their head.

I began the prayer.

"Dear Heavenly Father, thank you for the union, this fellowship. We ask that you bless the food we are about to partake and the hands that prepared it. Please cover us as we leave to depart for different destinations; get us all there safely. I ask a special prayer for Isabella and her grandmother and the rest of their family; give them the comfort they both need at this moment. In Jesus' name, we pray. Amen."

"Amen," Bobbie chimed in.

"Amen, beautiful Tyler," Lady T said.

"Oh, my goodness. This lobster macaroni and cheese is everything!" I said after taking my first bite.

Bobbie laughed. "I'm sure it's nothing like mine, but let me taste."

"Excuse me for a minute," Lady T said, easing out of the chair to answer her phone. Hello, this is Lady T," she whispered as she left the table.

"What do you think of the macaroni and cheese?" I asked Bobbie.

"It's pretty good. That chicken looks good too. Now, I wish I had that with my greedy ass," Bobbie said.

"You're more than welcome to have some of mine. Tonight is date night with Will and, with him choosing the restaurant, I'm sure it will be somewhere he can have a steak since I don't purchase beef or pork to bring in our home. I know I'll be having chicken tonight, yet again, or salmon, so please have at this," I insisted.

"Well, you don't have to twist my arm twice." Bobbie laughed, cutting half of my chicken breast.

Lady T arrived back to the table looking antsy.

"I apologize for that. I'm going to have to head back to the office. I have a situation with a tenant and a homeowner, ugh! Lunch is on me. A hundred and fifty should cover it, right? Tyler, box mine to go, and I'll come over tonight to pick it up. I'd like to see Will anyway," Lady T said as she dropped some bills on the table.

"Thanks, Lady T. Had I known you were buying, I would've ordered more," Bobbie said, laughing as she dug in.

"Girl, stand up and give me a hug. See your crazy ass later, and great seeing you, kisses," Lady T said hugging Bobbie then walking away. "Kisses, Tyler. See you and Will tonight. Love you," she tossed over her shoulder.

"Okay, thanks for lunch. Be safe and see you tonight. Love you more," I said, causing her to turn around and blow me a kiss.

"The time really flew by," Bobbie said, looking at her phone. "Mmmm, this is good, but I guess I need to get some to-go plates so I can get back to the truck." She forked one last bite of her food before waving over the waitress.

Asher reappeared at our table. "Yes, ma'am. I'm guessing you guys need to-go boxes?" he surmised.

"That's correct, three please, and you can bring the check as well," I spoke up.

"Will this be one or separate checks?" he asked.

"It will be one, please and thanks," I replied.

"Three boxes and the check coming right up. Do you need to-go drinks?" he asked.

"Not for me; you Bobbie?" I asked.

"Sure, a Coke to go with little ice, please," Bobbie responded.

"I'm going to run to the restroom right quick. Here's the money so he can go ahead and check us out," I said, getting up from the booth and walking to the bathroom to relieve myself.

"You and that bird bladder of yours," Bobbie said as I returned back to the table minutes later. "Asher already came and got the money. I'm waiting on the change," she said.

"Good. And, hush it right now about my bladder," I told her.

We laughed. Then, Asher reappeared at our table passing Bobbie the change, which she handed to me.

"Thank you both. I hope you have a great rest of the afternoon," Asher said with a cheerful smile.

"You're welcome and same to you," Bobbie and I said in unison.

"Let's get me back to my truck, so I will still have a job at 5:00," Bobbie joked.

"Yes, ma'am. We don't want you losing your job on my account," I said.

"Tyler, I want you to know that I'm here for you in any way that you need me to be. I support you, and I'm glad you have Will to be there for you as well," Bobbie said.

"Thanks, and you know that means a lot to me. That's why I wanted to have this conversation in person and not over the phone. I love you for being you, and because you are always there for me," I said, fighting back a tear that threatened to escape the corner of my eye.

"Oh, hurry up and let me in the car before you get all mushy on me," Bobbie said.

"Get in, Foxy Brown!" I said with huge laughter erupting from the pit of my soul. I truly loved my friend.

"Love you. Get home safely, and give my regards to Will," Bobbie said after we arrived at her truck. She closed the door and walked away. I looked at my best friend and smiled, truly glad to have a support system like my girls.

CHAPTER TWO

DILEMMA

"Good day, sir. Why haven't you called me?" Lashawn asked.

"Let me give you the long version, and hello to you, ma'am," I adjusted the phone to my ear and answered.

"Do you have a moment to finish our conversation from a couple of days ago, or will you use the 'I'm with a client' quote?" Lashawn grilled.

"Let me click over to tell Denise I'll call her back shortly after I speak with you."

"Okay and tell Denise hello and that I'll be calling her this weekend," Lashawn said, taking a softer tone when she spoke about Denise. That's how I knew we were about to bump heads.

I clicked over and said to Denise, "Hey, Lashawn says hello and that she will call you over the weekend. I need to catch up with her too, so I'll call you back shortly," I said.

"Okay. Tell her I'll be waiting for her call," Denise said before saying her goodbyes.

I clicked back over to Lashawn. "Now, I'm all ears ma'am," I told her.

"Let me start by saying I love you and want nothing but the best for you. If I came off a bit harsh or unsupportive the other day that wasn't my intention," Lashawn laid it out there.

"I know, and trust me, I felt your concern and love," I said.

"Good. Marriage is sacred, and I know that Will and Da Wife did it for benefit purposes and that you and he have hopes of marrying one day. I want that for you both and don't want you putting yourself in a situation that you can't turn back from," Lashawn said.

"I know, and I trust Isabella. It's only for the last wish for her grandmother, then we will have it annulled. Will is going to divorce Robin right behind me or around the same time," I assured her Will and I would have our day for our wedding bells to ring.

"Just two more questions, Tyler, and then, I'll let this go. How do Nell and Denise feel about this, and where will this wedding take place?" she asked.

"You know Nell supports anything that I do. She trusts I will make the best decision for me, even if it is on impulse. As for Denise, I will wait until I go home to see her and discuss it," I said.

"And where will this take place?" Lashawn asked again.

"We will be flying into Portugal, accompanied by Will as my best man, for her grandmother's birthday in July," I answered.

"Well, looks like you have it all figured out. Sounds like it will be an exciting trip for you all," she said, seeming to ponder it out loud.

"I think Will is more excited about the trip than me. He has made this all about his birthday month." I laughed.

"Now, that's what I want to see more of; you two being happy," Lashawn admitted. "But now that that's out of the way, when are you coming to see these sweet babies? They've been asking about you," she quizzed.

"I'm going to Tuscaloosa in two weeks for Talon's born day, so I'll plan to stay over with you and the kids for the weekend on my way back," I said.

"Sounds like a plan. I guess I'll get up from this bed now and get myself ready for work, so I will only be about seven minutes late," she said sounding a bit sluggish.

"Please ma'am. Get up and go to work. I need you to have a job so you can help me with my honeymoon," I said and laughed.

"Ha! Boy, bye. Love you," Lashawn said.

"Love you more. Have a good day," I said, ending the call.

Next, I called my sister, Nell.

"Hello," Latryce, my gorgeous niece, answered on the first ring as if she was expecting to hear from someone special.

"Hey there, how is my beautiful niece doing today? Is your mother home?" I asked.

"Yes, I think she's in her room getting dressed. How's my favorite uncle doing, when will you be coming home?" Latryce asked.

"Looks like in two weeks, so I can come to honor B's born day with her."

"Let me know. I want you to add some more color to my hair. I know it's going to be hard for her with this being her first year since my little brother has passed, I so miss his beautiful smile. Do you have anything planned?" Latryce asked.

"I miss him so much more, his beautiful smile and bubbly energy throughout the house. I am having t-shirts made with his picture on it and a quote on the back and getting a tomb topper for his headstone. He loved JR's Wings, so I thought we could do lunch there in his honor," I replied.

"That sounds nice; Nell will love that. I'm going to get some balloons and take over to his grave. If you need me to do anything, let me know, and I'd like a shirt in pink, please."

"I will order you one, but I don't really need anything. As for hair, I'm going to stay a couple of days so I will do your hair. Then, I'll head back to Atlanta," I said.

"Perfect, let me get her to the phone. I love you, and have a good day, unc," Latryce said.

"Love you more, and you too!"

"Nell, Tyler is on the phone," Latryce said as I heard her knocking on the door.

"Hello," Nell's voiced flooded the line, and I immediately picked up on her sadness.

"Hey, sis, how are you?" I asked.

"Taking it day by day," Nell sobbed.

"I know; it's hard. Try to be strong," I said trying to comfort her. "I can't believe it's almost been a year."

"Yeah, this year has really flown by. I miss him so much; I still can't believe he's gone," she said.

"Do you need me to come there now? You know I will?"

"No, I'll be fine. I wouldn't want you to drive all the way here. You do enough as it is," said Nell.

"I can never do enough. B was my baby, and I hurt and miss him, so your pain is unimaginable for me. Any way I can comfort you I want to offer it," I said.

"Are you going to come home for his birthday in two weeks?" she asked.

"Of course. I wouldn't be any other place than there with and for you, Nell."

"I love you so much, Tyler." Nell sighed.

"I love you more. I've ordered t-shirts and a tomb topper that I'll pick up next week. I was thinking we could go to JR's for the born day. Latryce said she's going to take some balloons over to put on his headstone; maybe we can all go together," I suggested.

"That's fine with me. I'm sure he's smiling down from above and would love that," Nell said.

"Nell, I wanted to talk with you about something, but I can wait until another time or when I come home in a couple of weeks."

"No, go ahead and tell me. I'm fine," she insisted.

"I have this Portuguese friend name Isabella whose grandmother is turning one hundred years old. Isabella would like to marry for her grandmother's birthday because she doesn't know how much longer she will live beyond this year," I blurted out.

"Oh wow, are you serious?" she asked.

"Yes, her grandmother's birthday is in July, and I'm going to fly with Isabella to Portugal and wed her in honor of her grandmother's last wish," I said.

"Really Tyler? I know Will is married to Robin, but how does he feel about this?"

"He supports me and will fly with us to Portugal to be there when I marry her," I supplied.

"What does marriage to her entail as far as honoring her grandmother's last wish?" she asked.

"The plan is to go to Portugal for her born day gathering. There will be a small ceremony at a small venue near their home. Her brother is taking care of all of the details, and he will give Isabella away. Will is going to stand in as my best man and one of her nieces that lives there will be her maid of honor," I shared the details.

"This really is a lot to process," Nell said.

"I know, sis. I decided to wait when I heard you were having a bad day. It will be a quick process, and we will be divorced before you know it," I assured her.

"I am sure you've thought this all through and talked it over with Will so know that I'm here as much as you need me to be. You're my baby brother, like a son, and I worry about you," she said.

"That's good to hear; thank you. I'm pulling up to the salon and about to start work. I just wanted to share this with you. I love you, stay strong, and know that B is in perfect paradise," I told her. Feeling the spirit of my nephew all around me, I smiled.

"I know, I love you too. Have a good day and talk with you soon," Nell said before hanging up.

CHAPTER THREE

ONE MORE TIME

On July 4, 2009, Will arranged a limo service to transport myself, him and Isabella to Atlanta airport for us to catch a flight to Lisbon, Portugal where he would be my best man as I married Isabella while there celebrating her grandmother's birthday.

"How are you feeling, Isabella?" Will asked.

"Anxious about seeing my grandmother and brother yet scared at the same time. This will be the longest flight I'll ever have to endure, not knowing if she will believe or receive this arrangement," she answered.

"You'll be just fine. You're going to have almost ten hours to sort your thoughts and emotions out and hopefully get in some rest," I consoled her.

"I will probably read some until I get sleepy. I booked my pod across from you guys' pod, so we'll be close during our flight," Isabella said, smiling reassuringly.

"I know you said we could stay at your family's house in the guest room, but I booked a room at a hotel nearby so it won't seem awkward," Will said.

I gasped. "You did what? Why?"

"Babe, it's no big deal. You and her family are meeting for the first time. That's awkward enough for everyone.

Add me to the mix, and it's too much. I used some points from our timeshare to get a room at a hotel that's less than a mile from their home," Will reasoned.

"Will, you didn't have to do that. My family will welcome you as they're going to welcome Tyler," Isabella assured us.

"I guess he has a good point though, so we will stick with his plan," I agreed. Will usually had a good sense of things, which made it easy to go along with his gut feeling about us not both sleeping in Isabella's parents' home.

"I trust you guys' judgment. I'm just grateful and appreciative you're doing this for me," Isabella said.

"Don't mention it," I said.

"I echo that," Will added.

"I will stay in Portugal for as long as grandmother wants me to stay. After our 'honeymoon,' I'll just tell her you have to get back to run your business," Isabella said.

"Whatever you need to do; I'm sure your grandmother will be happy to have you home with her celebrating her birthday and seeing her baby girl marry will be a dream come true for her," I said.

"I hope so. I think I'm going to nap a little then wake and read my book later," she said.

Will laughed. "I'm going to watch a movie. I know you're about to take a nap, as well," he said to me.

"You are wrong, sir. I am actually going to work on my business plan and our finances before taking my nap, now." I laughed.

"I know my babe too well," Will said.

"And, I bet you are going to watch Friday or Next Friday, right?" I joked.

"I am actually going to watch 'Underworld: Rise of the Lycans', sir," he affirmed.

Hours later, the flight attendant's voice awakened me from a deep slumber.

"Good morning ladies and gentleman. The pilot has notified us that we are about twenty minutes from the time the aircraft will descend. Please fasten your seatbelts and place your seats and tray tables in an upright position. We will come around to collect all disposable items. Enjoy your stay in Portugal," the flight attendant announced.

"I didn't realize how tired I was; I slept the entire flight," Isabella said with a yawn as she stretched.

"I managed to get all of my affairs handled before falling asleep. It was a great nap," I replied.

"You two slept beautifully the entire way. I watched both of you between movies and my nap," said Will. "Tyler, are you ready for the shenanigans? You meet your in-laws, and you marry your bride all in a matter of minutes?" Will chuckled.

"I'm sure it will be just as easy as your marriage to Da Wife. No shade," I said. Then, it was my turn to laugh.

"Low blow, but funny," he said.

"My brother just instant messaged me. He is at the airport awaiting our arrival," Isabella announced.

"What's the plan once we get there, Isabella?" Will asked.

"We can have my brother stop by your hotel to drop your luggage off then we head to meet grandmother; the wedding isn't for a few hours," she answered.

"Babe, you have the rings, right?" I asked.

"Fine time to ask, but yes I have them," Will joked.

"Don't be a butthole on my wedding day, sir!" I said, laughing.

"I'm going to run to the ladies' room, and I will meet you guys at baggage claim," Isabella said.

"May I kiss my companheiro bonito on his wedding day?" Will asked, calling me his handsome companion.

"I see you've been studying a little Portuguese," I responded.

"Yes, I have; I want to at least know some of the things being said while we are around her family," Will said in a husky tone as he inched closer to me. "Now, can I kiss you?"

"I don't know." I teased him. "Maybe…"

Will chuckled, giving me a look that let me know I would have to pay for teasing him.

"Maybe between what we both know we can hold a conversation with her family and residents," I switched the subject.

"I hope so," Will said just as Isabella rejoined us.

"Whew, much better! I see you guys got the luggage. Let's head this way because my brother, Tadeo, is waiting on us outside," she said.

"Right behind you!" Will said. It was comforting how supportive he'd been this entire trip. I looked at him as he walked beside me with a caramel dimpled smile, and I couldn't help but feel blessed.

"That looks like her brother over there," I said, pointing at a short and husky tanned gentleman who was scanning the area looking for us. His facial features were nearly identical to Isabella's.

"Olá, eu sinto sua falta irmão," Isabella greeted her brother by telling him how much she missed him.

"Eu também sinto sua falta, irmãzinha," Tadeo returned the same greeting with a hug.

"Ola' companheiro bonito, I'm Tyler," I said hello and introduced myself with my hand extended.

"Ola' e bem-vindo, Eu sou Tadeo," Tadeo welcomed us, extending his hand to me and then Will. "Avó espera," Tadeo said.

"Isabella, did he say grandmother awaits?" Will asked.

"That is correct, Will. You've really been studying your Portuguese," Isabella complimented Will for understanding her brother.

"Can we stop by Epic Sana Hotel so I can check in and drop my luggage off first, please?" Will asked.

"Tadeo, vamos pelo Epic Sana hotel?" Isabella relayed Will's question.

"Coisa certa," Tadeo affirmed he would stop by the hotel.

"The weather is very nice today for a wedding," Will spoke breaking the silence once in the car.

"It really is," I echoed.

"We are here, you guys," Isabella said once we pulled up to the Epic Sana Hotel.

"Will, do you want me to go in with you to help with your luggage?" I asked, giving him a heated look that let him know my true intentions.

"Sure," he answered.

"Be right back, you guys." I winked at Isabella.

"Tadeo, let's run over to the market right quick while they are checking Will in," Isabella said to her brother.

I caught up with Will as he was entering the building.

"Hey babe, we have time for a quickie. Isabella is going to stall Tadeo while we go to the room so that I celebrate my man's born day early," I said in a low husk.

"Good, because you owe me a kiss," Will replied.

"Welcome to Epic Sana!" the front desk attendant greeted us as we approached the counter.

"Hello, I have a reservation for Will Caldwell."

"I have you reserved for the presidential suite. Would you need one or two keys, sir?" she asked.

"Two please," Will said, sliding his credit card across the counter.

"Mr. Caldwell, I have you all checked in. The elevators are straight ahead. Take it up to the 27th floor, and you will be in room 2706. If you have any questions, my name is Renata. Enjoy your stay here in our lovely hotel and Portugal," Renata said with a bubbly smile.

"Come on, baby. Let me get you up to this room and hold you to your word," Will murmured.

As we stepped off the elevator, he immediately started groping and kissing me. He barely took his hands off me as he tried to open the door to the room.

"Hold on, babe. I'm going to give you the goods. Just get the room door opened."

He entered the room and pulled me inside behind him.

"I need you so bad," he said as he unzipped his pants.

Kissing him, I pushed him to the bed and began satisfying him orally. When I came up to kiss and straddled him, I said, "I want you to think about this tonight if I'm not able to be here in bed with you."

"Oh, Tyler, you feel so good. I love you so much, baby. Yes, just like that," Will moaned as he worked his way inside of me and began stroking.

"Oh, Will, just like that," I moaned out.

"Tyler! You feel so good."

"Kiss me! I'm getting close." I moaned as he kissed my lips. "Oh Will, deeper, deeper!" I yelled, and he obliged by pulling me down harder on his shaft.

"Hell yeah. That's it. Keep riding it, Tyler. I'm about to cum. Oh my God! Oh my God! Yessss!" he screamed, and his release erupted.

"Oh, I so needed that," I said after I let out an explosive release, joining him in ecstasy.

"We both did. That was a great welcome into Portugal," he added with a million-dollar smile.

"Lay still and let me go get a cloth to clean you up so we can head back down," I said.

"No, I'm coming in with you. We've got to hurry up and get back downstairs," he insisted.

"You're right; here's you a cloth," I said, pulling my pants up.

"Thanks, babe," he said.

"I'll grab your tux and dock kit and head on downstairs. See you in a few," I said.

"Alright, I will be right on down," he said.

Walking through the lobby, I caught Renata's eye and gave her a head nod before exiting the building. Just as I was walking out, Tadeo and Isabella pulled back up.

"Will is on his way down. Mind opening the trunk, Tadeo, so I can lay his tux back there?"

Tadeo popped the trunk, and I put the tux inside and hopped into the backseat.

"We ran to the market and got a few items while you were getting him checked in. Would you like a water?" Isabella asked.

"Sure, and thanks," I answered, reaching back to take the water as Will got into the car.

"Sorry for the wait, you all," Will said, his voice sounding like melting butter. *So sexy.*

"No worries; now let's go meet grandmother," Isabella said with a knowing smile.

Pulling up to Isabella's family house, I felt anxiety and numbness running through my body. I wondered if her grandmother would believe our story, or if she would question my sexuality or the mannerisms of her grandson-in-law. Though I tried to mask them somewhat, I could only be me.

"Okay, guys, we are here." Isabella looked back at us with a nervous grin.

"Let's do this, baby," I said, speaking to her adoringly for her brother's ears.

"Tadeo says you will change here and meet the pastor and the few family members and friends at the venue for our wedding. My gown is there, and I'll get dressed there while my niece does my hair and makeup," Isabella said.

"Voce pode mudra aqui," Tadeo confirmed what Isabella had just relayed when he opened the door for us.

"Obrigado," I thanked Tadeo, and he left Will and me alone to get dressed while he took Isabella to the venue to get ready.

"You alright, baby?" Will asked.

"Yes, just a little anxious, I guess," I relayed.

"I know there's a lot of anxiety built up in you being in an unknown country, meeting people for the first time, and having to play a role," Will sympathized. "But when you remember your purpose—"

"Having you here with me takes some of that anxiety away. Glad you're here for and with me. I love you, Will," I said, giving him a kiss that was interrupted by a knock on the door.

"Come in," Will said.

"Nos estaremos saindo em dez minutos," Tadeo said, letting us know we were leaving in ten minutes.

"Estaremos prontos em cinco minutos," I said, letting him know we would be ready.

"Esta' bem." Tadeo gave us a thumbs up and closed the door.

"Babe, will you fix my tie for me?" Will asked.

"You look so handsome; I can't wait until you divorce Da Wife and I annul my marriage with Isabella so we can have our dream beachside wedding," I said with a dreamy look in my eyes. I felt a wave of tears threatening to come to the corners over the thought of having a beautiful wedding with Will.

"It will all happen soon enough, and it will be magical, babe," Will assured me. His confidence brought a smile to my face.

"Alright looks like we are all set. Let's go before you make me tear up," I said.

"Tadeo, do you speak any English?" Will asked when we exited the dressing room and ran into Tadeo in the hallway. He was headed our way to get us, so turned around and walked toward the car when he saw us.

"Of course, I do. You guys seemed to be speaking Portuguese pretty well, so I thought you wanted to talk in Portuguese." Tadeo laughed.

"Whew, that's great English!" I said with laughter.

"You guys look really nice. How long have you two been friends?" Tadeo asked once we were in the car.

"Thanks, Tadeo, so do you. We've been friends about nine years," I answered.

"And how long have you known my sister?" he asked.

"About two years now, I think," I answered.

"When grandmother asks, tell her just over a year and that you knew she was the woman for you when you laid eyes on her, please."

"Whatever you need me to do or say," I assured him.

"Awesome, we are here. I will take you to meet with the priest as Isabella has already spoken with him," Tadeo said.

"Will, if you'd like, we can hang out in the city while they honeymoon tonight. Isabella told me you're celebrating a birthday soon?" he said as more of a question.

"Tadeo, don't you guys go out and get arrested tonight!" I said with laughter but also with a jealous heart. I knew I could trust Will, but Tadeo was extremely handsome and, with a little alcohol in his system, my man could be a bit flirtatious.

"Sure, hanging out with you will be cool," Will said.

"Let's go in here and get you and my sister married," Tadeo said with a smile.

When we entered the venue, it was beautifully decorated with hydrangeas throughout the reception hall. We walked through to get to the priest, and I noticed there was a long purple carpet for the walk of the bride and purple and gray ribbons alternating each chair for the guests.

"Whoever decorated this did a beautiful job; coincidentally our colors are used," Will said for my ears only.

"Yes, she asked my favorite color, and I told her to use these for the wedding. You alright with this?" I asked.

"At this point, I will have to be. Was just hoping I'd be seeing these colors at our ceremony," Will's voice cracked as he answered. That tiny bit of a falter broke my heart.

"Father Jeronimo, I'd like you to meet Isabella's fiancé, Tyler," Tadeo interrupted my thoughts, introducing me to the priest.

"It's a pleasure, Father," I said, shaking his hand before a quick glance back at Will who nodded.

"Do you mind if you and I have a word alone?" Father Jeronimo asked.

"Sure," I answered.

"Follow me this way." He led me into a big, roomy office toward the back of the church.

"Welcome to Portugal. I'm hoping your stay has been good so far."

"It has. Thank you."

"Good. I've spoken with Isabella and her grandmother, Sister Clarissa, and now I wanted to take some time to talk with you before I am to wed you both."

"Okay, I'm all ears, Father," I said.

"I just want to talk to you about marriage, share a few scriptures with you, and then pray over you before we go out to meet your bride," Father Jeronimo said.

There's a knock on the door.

"Father, I am sorry to interrupt, but grandmother would like to meet Tyler and have a word with him before she takes her seat," Tadeo said, ushering his grandmother into the room. Her beautiful olive skin, small five-foot frame, salt and pepper hair pulled up in a tight bun on top of her head struck me as much as her slow steps accompanied by a cane.

"Ola' avó," I said the respectful greeting "hello grandmother" and extended my arms to hug her. "Voce e linda," I remarked of her beauty.

Clarissa's tone was genuine when she responded, "Ola' meu filho prazer em conhece-lo," which means 'hello son; nice to meet you.'

"Prazer em conhece-lo," I said, letting her know it was nice to meet her, as well.

"Tadeo Ele e' bonito," Clarissa said.

Then, Tadeo looked at me and said, "She says you're handsome."

I smiled and thanked her for her kind words. "Obrigada avó." I turned to Tadeo. "Does grandma speak English?" I asked.

"Yes, I do, Tyler," Clarissa said, putting her hand over her blushing face. "Not as fluent as my grandchildren but pretty well. Thanks for marrying my granddaughter; I've never seen her so happy. Welcome to our family, and this is a beautiful way to celebrate my one-hundredth birthday," she said, opening her arms for a hug.

"The honor is all mine," I told her.

"Alright grandmother, let me take you to your seat, so Father can finish with Tyler. I hear Isabella is ready and guests are being seated," Tadeo said.

"Tadeo, where's Will?" I asked.

"He's sitting just outside this door awaiting you and Father to come," Tadeo said and walked out along with his grandmother.

"I am aware English is your first language, so what Isabella wants me to do is speak the ceremony in both languages to accommodate everyone," Father Jeronimo spoke up.

"Perfect," I said.

"If you'd like, you can grab your best man, and he can be in with us as I pray over you," the father offered.

"That would be great. I'll grab him," I said and stepped outside to wave Will in. "Come on in. He wants you present during prayer."

Once we stepped inside the room, Father Jeronimo began, "Please join hands. 'Father God, we thank you for this beautiful day and this wonderful occasion as I take one of your children to unite him in holy matrimony with one of my sisters of the church. Bless their union, their friends and other family members. Give them all the joy and happiness their hearts can hold. Amen."

"Amen," Will said releasing my hand, yet I could feel that he didn't want to let go.

"Amen. Alright, Father, let's get me married," I said.

Just moments after we stepped out "One More Time" started playing. Everyone stood up as my bride walked down the aisle to greet me wearing an ivory, bateau neck, trumpet gown and beautiful curls cascading her back just beneath her long veil.

"Please be seated," Father Jeronimo ordered the room.

The ceremony was beautiful but a blur. Isabella did a great job planning this from Atlanta, and we were both performing like Grammy-nominated actors. As I checked back into the events, I heard the words, "if anyone can say now why these two should not be married, let them speak now or forever hold their peace... If not, I now pronounce you husband and wife; you may kiss your bride..."

I raised her veil and gave her a closed mouth kiss, and we turned towards the audience, "I introduce to you Mr. and Mrs. Oliver," Father Jeronimo said, beaming with the pride of the father of Isabella's church.

We took pictures with her grandmother, brother, Will and Father Jeronimo. Then, we took some alone as guests were being seated in the hall for the reception.

"Congratulations and welcome to the family, Tyler," Tadeo said.

So many people walked up to us and gave their well wishes as we were led to our table. The reception ended pretty quickly as we noticed her grandmother looking fatigued.

"Isabella, your grandmother doesn't look too well. Maybe we should take her home to rest," I suggested. "Tadeo, come here." I waved for him to come over.

"Let's try to wrap this up and get grandmother home to rest. I don't want her to be too exhausted because we have to celebrate her birthday tomorrow," Isabella insisted.

Tadeo tapped his glass to quiet the room.

"May I have everyone's attention? Grandmother is not feeling her best, so we are going to take her home to rest as we are celebrating her hundredth birthday tomorrow and want her to be up to it. Tyler and Isabella would like to thank you all for coming out for this celebration. Please stay and enjoy the food and dance the night away," Tadeo announced.

"Will, help me get grandmother to the car please," I asked.

"Come on Mama Clarissa. Let's get you home to rest," Will said, making just as much of a fuss over my new grandmother-in-law as everyone else.

"You're the best," I whispered to the love of my life. Then, I turned to Isabella and suggested, "Make your rounds to apologize and say goodbye to your guests. We will get her to the car."

"Will do," Isabella said before walking off into the crowd and shaking hands.

"Good night everyone!" I announced, waving to everyone as Will and I exited to take Clarissa to the car.

"Are you okay?" I asked Isabella's grandmother once we got her into the car.

"Yes, I'll be fine, Tyler. Thank you for marrying my granddaughter. Now, I don't have to worry about her anymore. I know that she'll be taken care of," she smiled with a beam of light that made this entire trip worth it.

Standing beside me, Will patted my back. I remember looking into his eyes that night and seeing a man who I could go through anything with and still come out on top. I loved Will, and I couldn't wait to steal some time away so that we could be together to enjoy the city. Had I known Will would no longer be here three years later, I would have cherished our time together much more than I already did.

CHAPTER FOUR

Until the Pain is Gone

~March 2017~

"I will *kill* you!" Tristan yelled as he choked Peaches, her feet dangling in the air with each limb desperately trying to reach the floor.

"You're hurting me, Tristan. I can't breathe!" Peaches tried to pry away from his grip.

"Why do you make me do this to you? Why don't you just do as I say?" he yelled.

"Let me down, right now!" she said struggling to release herself from the tight clutch around her neck.

"I'm sorry, babe. I don't know what came over me," Tristan said when his eyes widened with the realization of what he'd done. Peaches fell onto the Australian cypress floors of their bedroom gasping for air.

"I can't keep dealing with your jealousy and insecurities. I'm over this!" Peaches yelled, picking herself up from the floor. She stumbled when she took a step toward the bed to sit down.

"When you are ready to talk about your behavior, I'll be downstairs in the basement. What I'm not going to do is stand here while you pretend to be the victim," Tristan uttered with an icy gaze that froze Peaches momentarily.

"Fuck you!" she mumbled under her breath. "I'm so tired of getting treated like shit."

Sitting on her bed, Peaches thought about her life and came to a few truths. She was done with being handled like she was Tristan's property. She had now, or she had never. She picked up her cellphone and dialed her father's number. It was a call she should have made a long time ago, but now that the moment of fearlessness was upon her, she dialed his number.

"Dad, I know you're probably asleep; I don't want to alarm you because I'm fine. Tristan has touched me for the last time. My car is packed, and I'll be heading to Atlanta sometime overnight when he falls asleep. I will call you when I make it there safely. Love you," Peaches left a voice message on her dad's phone then bided her time.

Tristan's loud snores wafted from the chair in the great room to upstairs causing Peaches' eyes to pop open. She had been lying in bed pretending to be asleep for an hour. She threw the covers off of her and said a quick prayer.

"Father God, please let me get out of here without him hearing me as I walk down these stairs," she whispered looking up to her ceiling. She picked up her phone and dialed her friend's number. "Hello?" Peaches whispered into her phone.

"Girl, are you alright? I've called you a few times today to see what's up," Sinclair said.

"Tristan came home acting a donkey. He accused me of everything under the sun."

"What's the plan? Are you still up for driving tonight or you going to wait until tomorrow when he leaves for work?" Sinclair asked.

"I packed my car earlier while he was gone out, and I put what I could in the trunk, so he wouldn't see my bags in it. Right now, I hear him snoring, so I'm heading out to the garage and will be getting on the road shortly. If I only make about two stops, I should make it to you in the morning before that Atlanta traffic gets crazy," Peaches said with a chuckle.

"Get out of there safely and call me once you're on the road. I'll be up awhile reading over a case," Sinclair said.

"Will do. Let me get out of the DMV, and I will buzz you then. Love ya, and thanks for being there for me, Sinclair," Peaches said.

"You're welcome, babe. Atlanta and I will be waiting on you to arrive," Sinclair said before the call ended.

"Good riddance, bastard," Peaches uttered as she closed the garage door to get into her cranberry Mercedes-Benz GLE-class.

"Peaches is everything alright over there?" her neighbor asked as she backed out of the garage. Her neighbor, Mandy, had come onto her lawn and was obviously concerned. "I heard some screaming earlier. Then, I saw you packing your car. Are you moving?"

"Thanks for checking, Mandy, but all is well," Peaches said, rolling her window up. *So much for catching a late night's breeze,* she thought as she pressed the button.

"Good. I wasn't sure if I needed to call the police," Mandy said before the window was all the way up. "You know I'm just two doors away if you need anything. We can take his ass out together," Mandy said with a wink.

"No need, Mandy; Tristan is asleep right now, and I'm heading to see a friend. Thanks for your concern. Have a good night." Peaches finished rolling up the window and pulled out of the cul de sac.

Peaches hoped Mandy would get the clue and go to bed instead of snooping around their house late at night. It did make her smile knowing Mandy was in her corner had she needed her.

"Hmmm, who am I in the mood to listen to?" Peaches browsed through her CD magazine as she ranted about Tristan. "God knows, I have dealt with his abuse and foolishness long enough. I am divorcing his ass. Come on Phyllis Hyman; help me with this journey to Atlanta for my new start," she said placing her CD in the player. Her phone rang just as the first song started. "Hello," Peaches answered.

"Hey there. Just checking on you to see how your travel is coming along?" Sinclair asked.

"Just popped in a CD and was about to call you to let you know I'm doing fine," Peaches said.

"I'll be up probably another hour or so. I want you to call me if you get tired or sleepy, and you should pull over to check into a hotel if you're too exhausted to finish the drive," Sinclair insisted.

"No, I'll be alright. I have to stay on my course because I need to get there, shower, and dress because I have an interview at Whiskey Mistress, so I can at least sing there until I find something permanent," Peaches said.

"Oh wow! You're not wasting time, are you? What time is the interview?" Sinclair asked.

"Well, when I said I was leaving today, I didn't know Tristan was going to do something to make that decision final. I was still hoping I'd come home and he would give me a reason to stay. But anywho, the manager and I both agreed on 10 a.m. Just as they're opening up to set up for the afternoon," Peaches said softly.

"Well, everything is happening as it should be, Peaches. Let me know if there's anything I can help you with to make your transition easy and smooth," Sinclair offered with sincerity in his tone.

"You're doing enough by opening your home to me. But you can help me file for divorce?" she said as more of a question.

"Of course, but that's a conversation we can have later. Let's focus on getting you here safely and working on starting a new life for you," Sinclair insisted.

"I hear you, but I know what I want to do and sooner is better for me," Peaches asserted.

"You know the procedures we will have to take, and I also want you to go sit for the bar so you can be the lawyer you were designed to be," Sinclair said.

"A conversation we will surely have soon, for sure," Peaches said, appreciating every word of encouragement from her friend. There was nothing better than having someone in her corner who breathed life into who she was destined to become. Sinclair was that friend to her. "Very soon," Peaches added.

"No pressure, when you're ready. I put your code in the gate and alarm keypad, so you'll have that when you arrive. I will probably be en route to the airport when you get here. I have to fly to Seattle in the morning but will be back on Sunday," he said.

"Sinclair, get some rest, and I'll be fine on the road. I have Phyllis playing and will make it to your condo in no time. Good luck on your case, and safe travels. I love you and want you to sleep tight," she said.

"Don't be trying to rush me off the phone, ma'am. I'm worried about you," he whined.

"I know you are, but I'm in a great place right now. I have my wonderful brother from another mother that I've loved since law school opening his home to me and giving me a chance at a new start in life," Peaches said. "What more could I ask for?"

"I don't know, but knowing that you're getting a new start, I'll be able to rest well then. Call me if you get sleepy, and I'll check on you when I get up to get ready for my flight. Love you, Peach," Sinclair said.

"Love you more, babe. Thanks for everything," Peaches said, ending the call.

✷ ✷ ✷

The next morning, Peaches walked in to ask for the manager for her ten o'clock interview. A beautiful blonde, six foot, lean-framed manager escorted her to the bar area and asked her a few questions about her background. Peaches allowed herself to become transparent, sharing that she grew up in the DMV area, raised by a single father after her mother abandoned her at the age of three to go off to be with a married man and raise his kids. Peaches was left to be raised by her father with the help of his sisters and later her stepmother. She shared she wanted a change of scenery and decided to move down south to hopefully make an album.

The manager immediately offered Peaches a position to sing at the Whiskey Mistress two nights a week after hearing her angelic voice singing Daley's "Until the Pain Is Gone."

"Order anything off the menu and have lunch on me," the manager said.

"I'll accept that offer," Peaches said and ordered the peach-glazed Alaskan grilled salmon with caramelized peaches over garlic mashed potatoes.

When Peaches finished having her lunch, she walked down the streets of Peachtree heading to her SUV that Tristan gave her for their third anniversary, she noticed there was glass next to the driver's door of her vehicle. She approached the vehicle to find the window had been busted out and there laid a rock on the seat. The car was a mess. The papers from the glove compartment were on the floor mat and passenger seat, and the CD/navigation system had been removed.

"Not today, Lord!" Peaches yelled, clasping her head. When she began to think straight, she took out her cell and called the police.

After waiting nearly an hour for the police to arrive to file a police report, she was over it. She took her car to the first Jaguar dealership she found, which was on Piedmont. Peaches was ready to trade her Benz to have a fresh start in this new city.

"Welcome to Hennessy Jaguar; I'm Monroe. Anything I can help you with today?" a tall, well-dressed black guy with a full beard and faux hawk haircut with the striking resemblance of James Harden asked as he approached her.

"I want to test drive the Firenze Red Jaguar XKR," she said.

"Alright then, a lady with style. Let me grab the keys and let you do a test drive. Care for a water?" Monroe asked.

"No thank you."

"What's your name, beautiful lady?"

"I'm Peaches," she said, blushing. "Nice to meet you."

"Go right ahead and get into your car. I'll be right back," he insisted. A few moments later, he returned with the keys. "Here you go, Ms. Peaches. Do you want to take a drive alone, or do you want me to accompany you to tell you all the wonderful features this vehicle comes with?" he asked.

"You can come along, but I know this is what I want," she said, and they both got into the car.

"Let's turn out and make the first right turn, then go down to the second light and make a left," Monroe guided.

"I love the way this seat is hugging me. Feels like one of my chairs at home," she said.

"A beautiful lady that knows what she wants and has great taste in vehicles. Should I tell you the features you're about to have?" he asked.

"Thanks for the compliment. You're not too bad on the eyes either, Monroe." Peaches chuckled and winked at him. "Go ahead and tell me the features."

"Keep this up, and you may get my employee discount, but we will have to keep that little secret from your husband," he jokingly responded.

"Soon to be ex-husband. That's why I'm getting rid of that Mercedes he bought me," she informed him.

"Today must be my lucky day." Monroe laughed.

"Maybe so, now for those features..." Peaches prodded.

"As you noticed, standard keyless entry and start system, active exhaust with quad tailpipes, Bowers Wilkins surround sound system, heated leather steering wheel, heating and cooling leather seats, and so many more features. I'm sure you feel how the wheels are gripping the pavement," he said.

"Yes, I do. We can actually head back now, so I can go change clothes and really enjoy this ride on the highway before this traffic you guys have here catches up with me," she said with a burst of laughter.

"Make a right turn, then go down two lights. We will make a U-turn, and the dealership will be on the right," he cheerfully instructed.

"Should I park here?" Peaches asked when she pulled in front of the building.

"Yes, let's get you in to finance while I'm getting your car detailed," he said.

"Just to let you know, I'll be trading my Mercedes. It has a window out that just happened a short while before I got here, and I'll be giving you a certified check. I'll need to run up to the bank once we get all the figures," Peaches said.

"Big Money! Look at you; you don't need my discount." He chuckled.

"Oh, yes honey; any amount I can save will do me just fine. I just relocated here this morning, and I just shared with you that I'll be filing for divorce soon. So, your discount is welcomed." She laughed.

"Do I at least get to take you out for a drink?" Monroe asked, and Peaches smiled. "I'll need you to fill out this form and a copy of your driver's license." He collected all of her information needed to process the sale and submitted it to the finance manager.

Peaches went to her Benz to gather all of her belongings while Monroe got her paperwork together. Once back inside, she signed all the necessary paperwork then went to her bank to get a certified check. When Monroe handed her the keys to her new ride, she said, "I gladly welcome and accept your request."

"Excuse me?" asked Monroe.

"How about tomorrow at 6 p.m. you meet me at Whiskey Mistress?" she asked.

"I look forward to seeing you tomorrow then, Peaches. Enjoy your new ride."

"Thanks. See you tomorrow, handsome." Peaches slid behind the wheel of her new car and spun out of the parking lot.

CHAPTER FIVE

LOVING YOU STILL

~October 2017~

"Good morning," I whispered as I turned over in the bed to greet Will, only to rediscover all over again that he was not there and never would be again.

Damn! I still can't believe it's been five years since you left me.

I looked at the alarm clock. It was only 4:21. Restless and listless, I crawled out of bed to walk across the cold, hardwood floors to the bathroom to empty my bladder so I could attempt to get some more sleep before starting my busy day at the salon.

Listening to sound of the October rain hitting my window, I grabbed my purple mink blanket from the bed and curled up on the sofa to watch *I Love Lucy* until the time came to take Sami for her morning walk.

My alarm sounded at 5:45 a.m. from the nightstand in the bedroom letting me know it was time to start my day. I got up from the sofa with my anxious, furry pooch scrambling across the floor rushing me to take her out as I threw on some sweats and sneakers.

As soon as we crossed the street, a burgundy Aston Martin pulled up beside us and stopped. I kept walking as the window slowly rolled down. I didn't know if I was about to be a victim of a drive-by or what. Before I could think of what to do next, a strong, distinctive voice said, "Good morning, sir." Something about the man immediately grabbed my attention, stopping me dead in my tracks.

"Good morning, handsome," I said flirtatiously, after taking note of the gentleman's appearance. I couldn't tell how tall he was although his voice made it seem as if he was as tall as the highest mountain. All I could see was his smooth, pecan complexion, almond eyes, freckles sprinkled throughout his nose and cheeks, and locs cascading just below his shoulder blades. I was having a moment like Gloria when she met Marvin in *Waiting to Exhale.*

"That is a beautiful dog," he commented. "What breed is it?"

"She's a miniature schnauzer; her name is Sami," I replied as Sami started barking uncontrollably at the mysterious stranger.

"How long have you had her?"

"Since she was a puppy."

"How old is she?"

Another question? I thought.

"She's fourteen years old."

He was surely asking a lot of questions from the comfort of his luxury sports car while I was on the verge of freezing on that chilly October morning. I needed Sami to handle her business so we could get back inside. I was still a tad bit skeptical of this man's intention. I didn't know if he was chit-chatting to be friendly or if he was going to kidnap me and sell me into white slavery.

"Do you mind if I step out a moment? I promise I'm not trying to hurt you," he stated as he quickly put his car in park and hopped out of the car without giving me a chance to respond.

I adjusted my hand in the pouch of my hooded sweatshirt to grip my pepper spray just in case he tried something crazy.

"Man, you're too sexy for me to try and harm you," he laughingly said.

Sami continued to bark at him while backing up on my feet.

"I'm Sinclair." He extended his hand as he walked toward me. "What is your name, handsome?"

"I'm Tyler," I said shaking his hand as I checked him out from head to toe. His voice made him seem like a mountain of a man, but the mountain gave way to a five-foot-five molehill. He was dressed in compressor pants that gripped his muscular thighs like a glove and showed his bulging eggplant. *Have mercy!*

My eyes quickly traveled upward, taking note of his abdomen. This brother didn't have a six-pack; it was a twelve pack, clearly defined and chiseled like a stone. Protruding through his athletic shirt, his pecs stood firm like a stallion in the night, and his nipples greeted me saying, "Hi." As I tried to avoid staring at them, I glanced down and noticed the beautiful ink work down both arms that invited me to squeeze them. I made my way back down to his feet; he was wearing Puma shower shoes. I went into a trance after I noticed his Morton's toes, and before I knew it, I was imagining them in my mouth. My trance was broken when he laughed.

"Tyler, why are you checking me out?"

"I'm wondering why you are out here on this chilly morning with no socks and no shoes to cover all of your forbidden…*fruit?*"

"Come on, Tyler. We are both men, and you know I had you at 'good morning,' sir," he said confidently. "How about you give me your number so I can let the anticipation build up in you until I decide to call?" He laughed again and gave me his phone that was in his left hand.

No, he didn't. This arrogant little mofo.

As much as I was offended, I was also intrigued and turned on even more. I took his phone and programmed my number in.

"I trust this is the right number," he said as I handed him back his phone.

"Yes, it is," I blushed coyly. "I wouldn't want you to do another drive by looking for me," I snidely remarked as I walked away with Sami, leaving Sinclair to his thoughts and already anticipating his call.

As I walked away, I noticed I had two missed calls from Alexis. While opening the door to let Sami in, my mobile rang for the third time. I quickly answered, "Hey, girl, I was just about to call you back."

"What in the hell has your sneaky ass been doing, you slut puppy?"

"I was out walking Sami." I laughed. "What do you want? Why are you blowing my phone up like a trick trying to get her daily dosage of wood from her situation?"

"I was trying to call you to give you some money by getting on your books today for a haircut and balayage color."

"What time do you have in mind? I'll tell you what; how about you come at two o'clock so you can take me to lunch after I slay your hair," I said as I placed Sami's food and water in the bowl.

"Two is perfect for me," she confirmed before shifting the conversation. "What kind of devilment were you in since I kept getting your voicemail?"

Chuckling hysterically, I said, "I was entertaining a handsome gentleman I met while walking Sami."

"Chile, you can tell me about that when I'm in your chair. I have a hot date with one of my little situations. He's taking me to the Future concert tonight," she explained. "Oh, by the way, your favorite male artist Kem is on *Good Morning America* right now."

"Girl, let me go so I can watch, and I'll see you at two o'clock. I love you."

"Love you too, bye."

I picked up the remote and turned on the television to *Good Morning America*. Kem was singing *our* song "Love Calls." I remembered the first time Will and I heard that song. We were shopping one Sunday afternoon at Shoemaker's Warehouse in Midtown for shoes to attend a dinner party later that night. Will took his mobile phone and used his Shazam app to find out the artist and song title playing through the speakers. From that moment, we became huge fans. Reminiscing on that day and seeing his live performance not only put a smile on my face but left me with a heavy heart.

There's nowhere to hide when love is callin' your name, yeah
From the dark, nowhere to hide, baby, yeah
There's nowhere to hide, so let love have its way with your heart

When love calls, love calls, love calls your name...

Love had called my name. Will and I had a love that only a few people in this lifetime are fortunate to experience. Love had called my name. Now, I was left all alone with nothing but my memories to keep me warm on lonely nights. Love had called my name. The man whom I thought I would spend the rest of my life with was gone, and there I was left wondering whether love would ever call my name again.

With Kem singing in the background and thoughts of Will in my mind, I got ready to face another day— without him.

After taking a quick shower and getting dressed, I ran by Target to pick up my copy of the new Kem CD. He'd sang a few tracks from his new album *Promise to Love* a few weeks ago when Lady T and I went to his listening party at Bar One. I decided, right then and there, I had to have that CD. With the CD firmly clutched in my hands, I was headed for the checkout lane when I heard someone snidely call my name.

"Hello, Tyler."

I looked up. I was surprised to see...*her*.

"Hello, Monica," I replied, trying to regain my composure. *Monica Johnston. Why the hell did I have to run into her today of all days? What the hell does she want?* It had been almost eight years since the last time I laid eyes on this chick at Da Wife's thirty-fifth birthday party.

"Long time no see," she said. "How have you been? I heard that you've written a book," she said as she stood with her arms folded, leaning on one leg and mouth perched. She didn't give me much direct eye contact, and I felt a sense of scolding and judgment coming from her. It was as if I saw the fumes coming from her ears as we spoke. Her purse was snuggled tightly under her arm as she stood rocking on her leg as if she was waiting for something to jump off.

"Yes, looks like you've heard of it," I sarcastically replied. "Have you read it?"

"Did you have to write a book?" she responded avoiding my question. "Couldn't you have just written it and not published it?"

How dare you question me on how to grieve or cope with the loss of my husband? I thought, which I knew showed up all over my face. She and Da Wife and Will's family knew what we had and meant to one another. Did I even have to explain myself? Not only was writing the book my coping mechanism, but I wrote it to encourage others to freely love whomever they chose.

"I wrote the book not only for my own healing but to touch lives and help others that have gone through the same thing I experienced when Will died. Although Will was married to Robin, I'm sure you remember he was my husband...too. You do remember the cruise we went on several years ago when he professed his love in front of you, Robin, and my family and friends on bended knee with ring in hand? How dare you stand before me and act as Robin and his family are acting, like our relationship never existed? By the way, I'm still waiting on my condolences from you."

Monica stood there looking at me, pondering how to respond. Just as I was about to walk away from the conversation, she uttered uncomfortably, "My condolences." Fidgeting, she blurted out, "I still think you and Robin should talk. After all, you were once friends."

No, she didn't!

Instantly, I became hotter than fish grease.

"She has my number, which has not changed after all these years. She can call if she sees fit. It was good seeing you. Have a good day!" I walked away before things went from bad to worse.

After checking out, I headed to my car. I was pissed with myself – not for what I said, but for the things I wished I had said to Monica. What Will and I had was LOVE, and it was no ordinary love. What Will had with Da Wife was on paper only. It was an arranged marriage that was only to last for a few years until he retired.

I also should've shared with Monica that I had forgiven Da Wife and Will's family. I needed to forgive them for my own healing, and I'd asked God to bless them. I moved on from the hurt and the betrayal. I was healing, focusing on my new salon, the scholarship foundation in Will's honor, and being the best Tyler I could be. I must admit that I really missed the friendship Da Wife and I developed over the years. I considered her family as I was sure she did with me. I was her Will, and she was my Grace. The flood of the beautiful memories we created quickly gave way to this dark moment in my soul.

Walking to my car, I became enraged and regretted not letting Monica have it right there in the middle of the aisle. I got into my car, opened the CD, and placed it in the changer. As Kem's soothing voice came through the speakers, tears started rolling down my face.

"Will, why did you have to leave me so early?" I yelled. "Robin, I wish you no harm, but I sure hope Karma has some mercy on you for betraying me like you have."

Sobbing heavily, I put my car in reverse to exit the parking lot to try to make the most of the day that Monica had ruined for me.

CHAPTER SIX

AFTER THE STORM

I'd been excited about this date with Eli for the past few weeks. I didn't think it was possible to entertain the thought of something serious with another guy again having been an emotional wreck since Will's demise.

Eli and I met on the gay dating app Jack'd. I liked the fact that he was open about his life. He shared every detail freely. I was apprehensive about doing the same. I wasn't sure how much of my life I wanted to share, especially so soon. Courting on the app had gone on for days until we decided to exchange numbers. We texted each other several times throughout the day, sending messages letting each other know how our day was going. Surprisingly, it felt right to me. He seemed perfect, standing just a bit over five-feet-nine-inches, about two hundred twenty pounds with nicely manicured hands, a beautiful smile, a voice that sounded as if he could be related to Barry White, perfectly formed calves with bow legs, and clean, pedicured pigeon toes. I received video messages throughout the day, and we'd FaceTime in the morning and before going to bed at night.

I arrived a few minutes before him at one of my favorite restaurants in the heart of Midtown in Atlanta, Einstein's. I was extremely nervous but excited at the same time. All kinds of thoughts ran through my mind: Would he find me attractive in person as much as in the pictures and video chats? How would he feel about me being an openly gay author of a novel that exposed my sexuality and details of my life with my partner of an eleven-year relationship and my aftermath experience of his death?

I stood off from the hostess stand waiting for his arrival and for the hostess to take me to our table. My mind was clouded with questions of whether I was cheating on Will. I wondered if Will would be bothered by the fact that I was getting back out on the dating scene. I somehow convinced myself to shake those negative thoughts and embrace what was in store for the night.

"I'm so sorry. Please forgive me for being late," Eli said after rushing over to where I stood waiting for him near the hostess stand. "I usually like to be early, so I can watch my date walk in." He laughed and leaned in to greet me with a hug.

Damn, he's fine. How can I not forgive him?

"All is forgiven," I quickly replied before adding an addendum. "But, this is your only pass for the next three-to-four dates, and we've got to get through this one first."

"Man, I know you've been really anxious to have this first one, so there will be a fourth, a tenth, a fiftieth date…"

I didn't know if he was confident or cocky. Either way, I was turned on by it. Taking a quick glance over him from head to toe, I noticed he dressed fashionably wearing a cream fedora, a chocolate cardigan, a pair of dark denim jeans, and python print driving loafers.

He chuckled as he folded the sleeves to his sweater. "Sir, you like my ensemble?"

"You look alright for a man that doesn't have a sense of timing. Do you own a watch by the way?" I chuckled as I shoved him.

"Those are some nice boots you have on, man. And that cardigan, is that from the Nene Leakes' collection?" he teased as he tugged at my sweater.

"Don't be a hater because I know how to *slay*. And you should be on time without having to make an entrance to get attention."

"Well, hopefully, they're not coming in here to shoot a scene from the Real Housewives of Atlanta because they'll be taping you and won't think about the cast for focusing on you sashaying," he said, laughing hysterically. "Let me stop before you walk out and not receive the pleasure of spending some time getting to know me," he chuckled as he grabbed me by the hand.

"You haven't earned the right or privilege to touch me yet, sir," I said flirtatiously pulling away.

The hostess informed us that our booth was ready and escorted us to the dining room. We immediately sat down and instantaneously locked eyes.

"Your beard looks nice on you, and your teeth are so even and pretty," I complimented.

"Thanks, man, wearing braces twice and sleeping in a retainer every night helps keep them that way, and I'll be sure to tell my barber he's doing a great job to have gotten your approval," he said with a broad grin, showing those evenly white teeth.

Our server greeted us. "Hello, I'm Josh, and I'll be your server. Is this your first time here? Would you like to hear our specials for the day?"

"No, we have both been here before. I'd like to have a dirty martini," Eli chimed in with a deep baritone voice.

"What do you recommend from the bar? I'll need something strong to sit through this evening with him?" I jokingly said to Josh as I winked at him.

"You should have the blueberry lemon drop martini," Josh suggested with a smile.

"The blueberry lemon drop martini it is. I would also like two glasses of water with lime, please and thanks," I said.

"We are ready to order our food too if you are ready to take the order, right Tyler?" Eli asked.

"Sure!" I responded.

"For starters, let us have your salt and pepper calamari and the fried chicken tenders," said Eli. "For my entrée, I'll have your pork chop, bone-in, with apple chutney over sweet mashed potatoes."

I skimmed the menu then ordered. "I will have the herb-crusted lamb chops with garlic green beans, red wine demi-glaze, and mushroom risotto."

After taking our orders down, Josh walked off toward the drink station.

"Again, man, accept my apologies for my tardiness," Eli began. "That move today got the best of me. This October rain and chill slowed my progress down a bit."

"Consider the apology accepted, sir. You could've easily canceled or done like most of these flaky dudes here and not show then call with a lame excuse two, or thirty, days later."

"Tyler, come on, you don't have to pretend with me. I'm sure your dating card, DM and voicemail are full of gentleman suitors trying to lock you down," Eli purported.

"I'm not going back and forth with you, Eli."

"Good, I'll just send them a silent 'thank you' for being fuck-ups," he stated as he tried to contain his laughter.

"I'm sure you keep watching the door behind me in hopes that your boyfriend or piece doesn't walk through and see you here on a date. This is a date, isn't it?" I asked, smiling sarcastically.

Eli laughed my question off, but he didn't answer it. After about ten minutes of talking about the day, his moving, and shooting the breeze, the server arrived with our water, cocktails, and starters.

"Do you mind if we bless the food?" I asked.

"No, I don't. You can do it."

I grabbed his hand and began to pray.

"Dear Heavenly Father, we come to you with bowed heads and humble hearts thanking you for the end of a beautiful weekend. We thank you for allowing us to get here safely as we ask the same as we depart for our destinations. Please bless the food we are about to partake and the hands that prepared it. Give us the nourishment our body needs. These and all blessings we ask in your son, Jesus, name. Amen."

"Whew, I didn't know I was on a date with a deacon, minister, or elder," Eli remarked, laughing while still holding my hand. "I'm just kidding. Beautiful grace, sir."

I laughed. "Ahh hush! I'm trying to pray all of your sins away."

Eli then picked up his martini glass to raise for us to toast. "Here's to a wonderful night. May we both receive what we need from this gathering. Cheers!"

We tapped the tip of our glasses before sipping on our cocktails. While we were eating on our starters, we had some very stimulating conversations.

"Tyler, at first, I was apprehensive about meeting you. I thought I was being catfished," Eli confessed. "When you sent pictures of yourself, I thought you were a model whose pictures were being used by some random guy playing me, and as we exchanged information, I looked you up and recalled seeing your book at my best friend's house."

"That's a first. I've never had anyone tell me that," I said sipping my cocktail.

"Mister, I am trying to pick up on this accent of yours. Where are you from?" Eli asked.

"I'm from a small town in Alabama just outside of Auburn and between Birmingham," I replied.

"Okay, I can hear that southern belle in your voice, but you talk so fast I would have guessed you were a northerner." He chuckled.

"Do share where you are from, sir, as I know you're a transplant to too," I stated then anxiously awaited his answer.

"I'm originally from South Carolina but relocated here from Philly after finishing college. My mother is still in South Carolina, my father is here, and my sister lives in Florida. I'll give you my social and the rest of the family tree if you get to date number two," he added with a coy grin on his face.

"You've got jokes, funny man," I said, calling him out on his behavior before asking, "How does your family feel about your sexuality?"

"Well, my mom, grandmother, aunt, sister and cousins all have supported me from the time I decided to let them in that part of my life. It was my father that struggled with it at first, but our relationship has grown stronger, and he's accepting and supportive of my choices," Eli stated with pride. I could tell that having a good relationship with his father was important to him. "What about you? How does your family feel about it?" he asked.

"I don't think I ever recall *coming* out. They've always felt it, and it has been accepted. Now, my late grandmother wasn't really having it. She had me up in church preaching, singing, leading the communion, you name it." I laughed.

"I bet you were the biggest butterfly in school, weren't you? Had the boys running behind you in the locker room and shower?"

"I was Queen of the Ball. My milkshake brought the boys to my yard, locker room, dirt roads, you name it," I affirmed with laughter and sarcasm as I rolled my eyes at him.

"Seriously though, Tyler, you seem like a cool guy. I know this is a bit premature, but I'd like to see you again and again and again."

"Let's see how you act the morning after. You know how you guys get amnesia after the first date."

"Man, don't be trying to play all hard with me. You want a second date with all of this sexiness so you can take me off the market," Eli hinted, indicating he really wanted to see me again.

Before I could respond to his humor, the server, Josh, approached us asking if we'd like anything else as the bar was about to close.

"No, I think I'm done, but you can bring the check if you don't mind," said Eli.

"Will it be one or two checks?" Josh asked.

"You can put them on one," Eli responded.

"Excuse me, sir. Will you put the appetizers and drinks on one and the entrees on the other?"

"Sure," Josh said, then walked away to settle the check.

"Hmm, a gentleman. Now that's impressive. I didn't expect you to do that, but I'm glad to see you're not a moocher like most guys out here looking for a free meal," Eli said.

"I think it's only fair I contribute since we both kind of agreed to see one another. Now had you asked, or I asked, the proper thing to do would be for the person who asked to pick up the tab in hopes of the other leaving a tip, I'm guessing."

Josh returned with the split checks and took our cards to close out our tickets.

"What are you doing with yourself the rest of the night since I've gotten you full on cocktails, food, and you're on a natural high from looking at me?" Eli's arrogance got the best of him again.

I looked at him slyly. He was one to watch.

"I have to go walk my dog and look for a place to meet my friends for brunch after church in the morning," I replied.

"I was going to propose that we go to a coffee shop to talk some more as I'm not ready to go home nor want this night to end."

"Well, I really need to go walk Sami. It's been several hours since she's been out… I *would* invite you to my house, but I would rather we wait a few months before entertaining at one another's home."

"I'm in agreement with you on that, Tyler, because I'm so into you right now that I can't promise you I wouldn't try to steal a kiss from you or …" Eli chuckled blushing like a schoolboy. "Tyler, I know this is premature to say this. I will go at any pace you'd like. All I ask is that you just be open to giving us a chance."

I smiled, taking in Eli's request as the waiter handed us our cards. We both signed the receipts. We left the restaurant and walked over to the valet to wait for our cars. We were both silent because the night had already said so much.

"Let me grab the door for you, sir," Eli uttered as the valet driver pulled up in my car.

Hmmm, he's a gentleman, I thought.

"Thank you!" I replied as I eased into the driver's seat.

"Call you when I get home," he assured me.

"Okay!" I smiled. "Bye!"

As I drove down Juniper with Eli fading the distance, I had this funny feeling in the pit of my stomach. What was it? It took me a moment, but it felt like the seeds of love I hadn't felt since the day I met Will. Optimism was very heavy in the air. I replayed our dinner conversation in my head over and over again. Eli and I had so much in common, but we were different at the same time. I felt so comfortable that the guilt I had for entertaining the thought of another man in my life wasn't as heavy on me anymore… I needed this.

CHAPTER SEVEN

FREE AS A BIRD

I woke with the sun beaming into my window and onto my face. I felt peaceful yet anxious to check my phone to see if Eli had called or texted me. I played our conversation from last night over in my head as I laid there thinking about the timbre of his deep voice. I envisioned exquisite details of a dream wedding and being that fortunate guy he'd marry. I was a confident guy and loved the skin I walked, breathed, and lived in, but I still couldn't believe Eli was interested in me. I figured he would be interested in guys that looked and talked like him. Yet, he instinctively knew what to do to make me feel like I was the only guy in the world. I dreamt of what it would be like to fall asleep next to him at night and wake up in his arms in the morning. With the warm sunrays penetrating my skin, I could lie in bed and fantasize about Eli all morning, but I had to get up and go give praises to the one that brought this seemingly wonderful man into my life.

On the way to church, I was excited to receive a video message from Eli.

"Good morning, Tyler," he began, giving his cute signature wave. "Thanks for a lovely evening—dinner, conversation, everything. All of it made me want to spend more time with you. I'll be doing laundry and going to Joe's on Juniper later to meet with one of my close friends for wings and drinks. I would love to see you while in I'm in Midtown afterward, that's if you're available."

Eli's message made me feel like a giddy little school boy. I just couldn't believe it. Finally, I had found someone I could possibly love again. I couldn't help myself, but I had to share what I was feeling with Will.

"Will, I miss you so much and love you with all of my heart. I've met someone, and he's really showing me chivalry, interest and other qualities that I'm sure you'd want for me. I'm asking for your blessings as I take this journey to see where it leads." After saying that prayer, I decided to let my wall down and be vulnerable and open to whatever life would bring my way during this 'getting to know you' phase. I had hope that Eli would be a good person.

I pulled up to Hopewell Missionary Baptist Church and parked in the second parking area furthest from the church. I could feel the breeze hitting my face and the wind blowing the tail of my sports coat as I approached the church. I was home within the walls of this church, and I couldn't wait to get inside to praise God for his blessings.

* * *

A few weeks later, a drunken Eli sent a video message from a restaurant.

"Hey, Tyler, I'm here at Joe's with my friend Lamont, and I'm so tipsy. I don't think I should drive home. Maybe you should come get me and let me lay in your arms until I am sober. I may slob a little on your back, and my dick may get erect, but I promise not to try anything. What say you?"

Chuckling, I shook my head. Then, I replied with a video message as I reached the lounge where I was meeting Lashawn.

"Hey Eli, as tempting as the invitation is to come meet you and Lamont, I already have plans to meet my niece and friends out for a celebration tonight. Call me when you're free later." I valeted my car and hurried inside to find Lashawn waiting on me and others to arrive.

"Hey, love, you look beautiful this evening," I greeted her.

"Thanks, Tyler, you look quite dapper yourself. Have you heard from any of the girls?" Lashawn asked.

"No, I haven't spoken to any of them. But I'm sure they're on their way," I replied.

The hostess told us she'd take us to our table and would bring the remainder of our party to join us once they arrived. As she led us to our table, I tuned in to the vocals bouncing off the walls of the room. I could feel every decibel in my soul.

"It's true. I'm leaving my bags are at the door. You and I, we can't make it. We can't make it no more," the singer sang into the mic, and at the time I didn't know she had been reminiscing what she had to do almost two years ago. Since leaving her marriage, she poured her heart into her passion—music. She sang her heart out every Sunday night at Whiskey Mistress. The way she sashayed across the stage with those beautiful golden curls, petite frame and powerful lungs that would bring the angels from Heaven and enamor them with her melody, it was awe-striking. The audience sat in awe wanting more each and every week.

On this Sunday night, she performed the song "Give Me One Good Reason to Stay" by the late Phyllis Hyman. Bobbie, Denise, and Alexis made their way to our table as Lashawn waved them to our direction. After greeting each of them with a huge hug, I immediately tuned out my dinging phone and gave my attention to my best friends and niece as we were all out celebrating my niece's new freedom.

We had been hanging out for a while when Lashawn asked the server, "Could you bring us another round of vodka and pineapple juice, and put it on my uncle's tab?"

"Yes, bring them all another round, please," I said to the server. I stood up and made my way to introduce myself to the singer. "Hello, beautiful. Your voice is so captivating that I still feel the chills on my arms," I shared as I extended my hand to her.

"Honey, I don't do handshakes. I do hugs. I'm Peaches and thank you for the compliment. I hope you will enjoy the next one I sing," she said with an infectious smile.

As she pulled me into a hug, I said, "Well, if you keep going at it like this first one, I'm certain I will. I'm Tyler by the way."

"This is my first time seeing you here in the crowd. Are you visiting or a local?" Peaches asked.

"I live here. I brought my sister/niece and a few girlfriends out tonight to celebrate her divorce," I said.

Peaches chuckled as she fixed her dress. "I need to come in and be a part of that celebration!"

"My apologies for the interruption, but sir, we are waiting on you to come and sit with us and let this lady get back on stage and sang!" Bobbie said as she nudged me in the side.

"Peaches, I'd like you to meet Bobbie," I said introducing the two.

"Bobbie, it's a pleasure meeting you and congratulations on the divorce!" Peaches said beaming like a Cheshire cat as she leaned in to give Bobbie a hug.

"No babe, that's not me. It's Tyler's niece, Lashawn, that we are celebrating. I'm a newlywed," Bobbie acknowledged as she gave Peaches her hand to shake. She was still in marital bliss, and it oozed off of her.

I cut Bobbie the side eye, letting her know I was wrapping it up so to give me a moment.

"Peaches, I'll let you get back to entertaining your fans. Please come by our table and have a drink on me so I can introduce you to the rest of the girls," I said once Bobbie walked away.

"Thanks, Tyler, I may take you up on that," Peaches said.

We had stood there for a few more minutes chatting it up as if we had known one another for years. It was my first time at Whiskey Mistress, and it was on the recommendation of a good friend. I assured Peaches I would be coming back since I was so moved by her voice and overall appearance on stage.

I looked down at my mobile and noticed Eli was FaceTiming me.

"Excuse me, Peaches. I have to take this call," I said before walking into the restroom to speak with Eli a moment.

"Hey there, sir. How is it going with you and the girls' night out?" Eli asked, slurring a few of his words.

"I really haven't had a chance to fellowship much since all of them arrived. We must come back together one Sunday night so you can hear the lovely vocals of this songstress, Peaches." I said.

"Cool, I'd like that. I'm not going to hold you from them. If you're not too tired when you leave, I'd like to see you tonight." A look of desire flashed in his eyes before he added, "Have fun, sir!" He waved, blew me a kiss, and ended the call.

I walked out of the restroom to join my party to continue the celebration. The energy was high, and all were in great spirits.

"It's about damn time! I recall this night is supposed to be about me," Lashawn pretend cried with a slight attitude.

"Calm down and sip your drink, ma'am, so that I can propose a toast to you," I offered along with a tip of my glass.

"Whatever! I need another one on its way since I've waited for you to get your ass back over here so that I can have my moment," Lashawn whined. She was in straight diva mode, and I couldn't help but chuckle a little on the inside.

"Glasses raised ladies!" I roared, getting everyone's attention. "Congratulations to Lashawn on her newfound freedom and to Bobbie for the birth of my beautiful little niece." We all toasted, clinking glasses together and smiling.

"Shit, can't I just have a toast all by myself without having to be included with Bobbie and the birth of her little one?" Lashawn jousted.

"Girl, congratulations on the beginning of a new chapter in your life. I am so happy for you, and I am right behind you. My husband finally agreed to sign the papers! So, cheers." Alexis stood and held her glass up. We all burst in boisterous laughter before continuing the celebration. Drinks flowed plentifully among us. Everyone was in a good mood.

"Tyler, so what's the singer's name you were over there all kissy with?" Denise asked.

"Her name is Miss Peaches," Bobbie cut in.

"He will be having some kind of function soon and have her up in there singing, so you all get ready for your invitation," Denise teased, and they all laughed at the shady comment.

"Ladies, matter of fact, I'm going to offer her a hair consultation to get her in the chair and then lay it on her that I want her to be my new best friend, ha!" I said before excusing myself to the lounge area to answer my vibrating phone. "This is Tyler."

"Good evening, handsome, I hope that I didn't catch you at an inconvenient time. You gave me your number two weeks ago," Sinclair's smooth voice said into the line, eliciting a smile from me.

"Sinclair, it's great hearing from you, man. I'm out with my family. May I call you tomorrow afternoon?" I asked, knowing without even turning around that my girls were shooting daggers my way and probably trying to eavesdrop.

"I'll pencil you in," he said. "I look forward to speaking with you, Tyler. Enjoy your evening," he told me and hung up.

I walked back from the lounge area of the bar as Peaches was finishing "Free as a Bird." She was such a beautiful songstress.

"This song is dedicated to my new friend, Tyler," her sultry voice called out as she waved in my direction.

I smiled, waving back at her.

"There he goes y'all. She will be his new best friend now," Denise said, cutting into my moment with Peaches. She was probably right. Peaches would soon be my new best friend. Denise grabbed her stomach and laughed aloud.

"Funny Denise," I said, taking my seat back at the table which was filled with some of my best friends.

A few minutes later, Peaches joined us at our table.

"Good evening ladies. How are you all?" she said, waving at everyone.

My crew greeted her with smiles and waves back.

"Thanks for the dedication, Peaches. I love that song by Vivian Green, and you really do it justice," I complimented.

"You're welcome. I wanted to come over and congratulate your cousin on the divorce," Peaches said.

"Lashawn here is my niece, Peaches." I pointed toward Lashawn.

"Thank you, Peaches! You have some beautiful vocals. Why don't you join us in celebration of my night?" asked Lashawn.

"I will do just that. I appreciate the warm welcome. I know how you feel to be free of that kind of a burden because I have been there. Cheers to you." Peaches raised her glass to toast Lashawn.

"Peaches, how often are you here performing? I'd like to come hear you again," Bobbie asked.

"I'm here every Sunday night and typically perform two to three songs. And as you can hear, the live band plays for the remainder of the night," Peaches replied.

"Well, you have a beautiful voice, and I love that dress. Where did you get it from?" Denise asked.

"Neiman's; thank you," Peaches replied.

"You're welcome." Denise continued to admire Peaches' dress.

"Jared, will you take Tyler and his party up to the Marilyn's Retreat and give them anything they'd like?" Peaches asked the server who was now hovering over us.

"Lashawn, look at you with the royal treatment. The night is about you, after all," Alexis teased.

"You mind bringing me the tab up there, so I can cash out? When you take us to the Marilyn's Retreat, we'll have a round of Patron shots, your lemon pepper and teriyaki whiskey wings, zucchini fries, and boom-boom shrimp?" I told the server then grabbed our drinks and exited from our table.

"Yes, sir. I will bring it right up," the server replied. He then guided us to Marilyn's Retreat where we had a wonderful time for the next few hours.

As the night came to an end, the four ladies were hugging one another to say their goodbyes, while they were out at the valet awaiting their cars. I gave my niece the fob and key to my place after deciding I was going to stay the night with Eli.

I made my way over to Peaches and said, "Goodnight Peaches. It was such a joy hearing your voice and spending time with you. You didn't have to do that, but I appreciate your gesture. Please take my card and come let me show that beautiful hair some love on me."

"Oh, Tyler. I will definitely take you up on your offer, and anytime you are here I will make sure you enjoy yourself. Deal?"

"Sounds lovely to me." I hugged her before leaving.

*** * ***

"Hello?"

"Good morning, Tyler, are you available to meet for brunch today so we can talk things out?" Robin asked. It was Monday morning around 8:42, and Da Wife wanted to have brunch. I had been expecting this call.

"Sure, I can do 11:30. Do you know where H. Harper Station is off Memorial Drive?" I asked.

"No, I don't, but I can Google it and meet you there. And 11:30 is good with me," she replied.

"See you soon." I pressed end on the call and removed my foot from being wrapped around Eli's leg as I woke him with a kiss on his forehead.

"Morning, babe. It's time to get up so you can start preparing for work," I suggested.

"Uhhhhh, what time is it? Will you give me just ten more minutes please?" Eli mumbled.

"Okay, ten minutes," I said crawling from under the cover to grab my clothes from the mahogany colored leather chaise in the corner of his bedroom.

As I walked into the bathroom, the motion light came on, and music started to play. I reached for a disposable toothbrush in the drawer of the vanity and began brushing my teeth before cleansing my face. Finished freshening up, I walked back into the room to wake him up again.

"Alright now, sir, your ten minutes are up. I brushed my teeth and cleansed my face a little longer to give you an additional eight minutes. Now get up!" I stressed.

"Lay with me for five minutes," Eli pleaded, pulling me on top of him in the bed.

"Babe, let's get up. I have to go home to shower. I'm meeting Robin for brunch this morning, and I don't want you late for work. Let's start moving." I pulled off of him and got out of bed.

"Will you start me some coffee and put a bagel in the toaster for me before you head out?" he asked.

"Sure, I'm certain I can find my way around your kitchen to meet your request," I said as I leaned in to give him a kiss on the forehead.

"The bagels are in the bread box to the right of the toaster, and the coffee and mugs are just above the Keurig in the cabinet," he said crawling out of bed.

"Text me after you've safely arrived at work," I yelled after Eli as he walked into the bathroom to shower. I walked down to the second level to the kitchen to start the Keurig, putting the mug on it and loading the K-cup just before I pulled out a saucer for him to put his bagel on. Then, I locked the door as I was leaving.

I opened my car's sunroof and put on my sunglasses before gliding onto I-20 headed to my condo in Midtown.

"How did we ever lose our minds and fall apart knowing we're the only to heal each other's hearts?" The lyrics of Gregory Porter's song "Insanity" chiming out of my speakers were interrupted by my ringing cell.

"Hello."

"Ahhh sir, where are you, and when are you coming home? I am ready to get on the road," Lashawn yelled.

"I'm getting off the exit now, ma'am. Be there shortly. Will you meet me outdoors with Sami so I can walk her right quick?" I asked.

"Sami has been walked and fed. Why do you have that damn music so loud?" Lashawn uttered.

"Thanks, see you shortly, and stop trying to regulate my ride." I laughed.

When I made it inside my condo, Lashawn and Denise both looked like they were ready to run me over to get out the door.

"Good morning sir, glad you could make it in to see us off. You owe Lashawn some money for walking your overbearing and barking dog," Denise said and chuckled.

"Hello, my little fat baby. Did they treat you well while I was gone?" I leaned down to give Sami a hug and pet her.

"Yes, we treated her very well, sir. Can you at least go up in the parking garage and get the car then take our luggage out for us for taking care of your baby?" Lashawn hinted.

"Yes, if you will, press the wrinkles out of this shirt for me right quick while I go get your Jeep."

Lashawn huffed out a deep breath. "I guess that can be handled for you, sir."

I walked out to the parking garage to drive the Jeep down. When I was done, I locked the doors and opened my front door to yell, "Ladies, the vehicle is in the alley. Where are the bags?"

"They're sitting outside your bedroom door," Lashawn screamed.

"What are you doing the rest of the day, Tyler?" Denise inquired.

"I'm about to shower then meet Robin for brunch."

"Wait a minute, what? Why are you meeting Da Wife after all she's put you through?" Lashawn questioned.

"I saw her friend a few weeks ago, and she suggested we talk. I'm guessing that's why we are meeting," I supplied. Though I was ambivalent about meeting Da Wife again, I hoped it would give me some closure.

"On that note, sir, I will say my goodbye. Love you, Tyler. Hope you get what you need from this meeting," Lashawn whispered in my ear.

"Love you, guy. I'll call you when we make it home. Tell Robin hello for me," Denise added.

I gave them both a hug then walked back inside to shower.

✶ ✶ ✶

Da Wife and I pulled up at the same time. I waited for her to park and get out of the car. We exchanged hellos and a hug and walked into the restaurant. I informed the hostess of the reservation for two in my name. The hostess immediately took us to our booth and menus were given to us as well as the specials for the day. We nodded in unison as we glanced over the menu and ordered drinks for starters. Our small talk was awkward as expected.

"How did you find this restaurant, and do you know where the restroom is?" she asked.

"It's just a little place I come to sometimes," I responded then pointed in the direction of the restrooms.

"Well, it's nice. I'll be right back," Da Wife said.

As she excused herself, I texted Eli to let him know I had made it and it was going fine.

Eli responded back, "I forgot to say, 'Happy one month anniversary, and I love you..'"

Then, I silenced my phone, so there would be no interruptions. Da Wife returned from the ladies' room and gave me a smile that one might receive from someone passing down the grocery aisle to be courteous.

Robin sat down about the time our server returned to the table with some peach cornbread muffins and water. "Are you guys ready to order," she asked.

"Robin, if you're ready, I'll let you order first," I said.

"You can go ahead as I skim over the menu a couple more minutes to decide what I'd like," Da Wife countered.

"I'll have your crab cake eggs benedict with a side of cheese grits and a mimosa with pineapple juice, please and thanks," I ordered.

"Ma'am, are you ready?" the server asked Da Wife.

"Yes, I'll have your salmon croquettes, two eggs poached, breakfast potatoes and a cup of coffee."

"I'll get this right in for you." The server smiled before walking away.

"I will open the floor for you to begin," I cut to the chase, allowing her the opportunity to start off the conversation to get what she needed off her chest.

"I want to begin with how hurt and disappointed I am with you for not being there for me when I suffered the miscarriage of my baby. You were to be the godfather of my daughter," she said, her voice trembling. After a brief pause she continued, "Tyler, I wanted you to hurt from losing Will like I hurt when I miscarried my pregnancy."

"Robin, I want to apologize if you felt I wasn't supportive or sympathetic enough during your loss. I had just relocated and started a new job. There was no way my boss was letting me off to be there for you, but I wanted to desperately."

"Had I not called you to inform you of Will's passing, would you have called me?" she asked.

"Honestly, I can't say that I would have because you didn't cross my mind. My first thought was to call his parents and family. Having to deliver that news was a tough call to make to all of them," I admitted.

"After I got home and got the news, you were my first thought. His parents weren't a second thought at all," she confided.

"Robin, we could go back and forth all morning about how things could've been done differently, but it won't bring Will back. Yes, I should have been your first thought because my relationship with Will is why this agreement of you two getting married came about.

His family didn't know you two were married," I reminded her.

She opened her mouth to reply, but the server placed our plates in front of us interrupting her.

Once the server left our table, I reached for Da Wife's hand. "Would you like for me to bless the food?"

"Sure, that would be nice." She offered her hand for prayer.

"Dear Heavenly Father, thank you for the opportunity to see another day and a chance of being great. Bless the food that has been placed in front of us and the hands that prepared it. Give us what we need from this meeting. We thank you in your son's name. Amen," I said.

"Amen," she chimed.

"They shipped Will's possessions to me. It was too costly to continue paying for the storage of all his belongings, so I sold and gave away most of his things. But I have a box of Will's things I gathered for you," she said.

As I sat in disbelief of what I was hearing, all I could think of was the woman that sat across from me once was a dear friend that seemed like family to me. My mind was puzzled trying to figure out why I never received the phone call to tell me of the storage or to ask how I wanted her to handle Will's belongings.

"Shouldn't I be the one deciding what to sell or give away?" I seethed.

"Well, I guess like I wasn't the first thought when I lost my child, I applied the same with Will's things," she answered, spewing a little venom in her tone.

I held back tears. "Call me when it's a convenient time for me to come by to pick the box up then."

"I'll be traveling a lot the next couple of weeks, so I will check my calendar and get back with you," she retorted.

"Thanks, I'll wait to hear from you, Robin."

"Tyler, I would be remiss if I didn't say one last thing to you about why I have so much resentment towards you!"

"Please share, Robin."

"When I called you shortly after I had the miscarriage, you were going through security at the Hartsfield-Atlanta airport to board a flight out of the country, and I was here grieving the loss of my baby," she sobbed.

"I had no idea that you were harboring such feelings towards me for a trip that I had planned even before I relocated to Texas," I remarked.

"I've been there for you on many occasions and thought you would've postponed your trip knowing that I needed you at that moment," she said.

"Robin, if there was any way I could have, I would have done just that. I'm sure you're thinking that I couldn't come to be with you after you miscarried, but I could go on a trip, and—"

"Truthfully, that's exactly what I was thinking with a broken heart," she cut in.

"For whatever it's worth, I cried when I got the call. I was so looking forward to holding your baby, although you deviated from the plan of you, Will and I having one together," I admitted.

"Now, I know how you feel, and I really needed to get that off my chest. I'll be in touch soon to have you get the box of his things I have for you," she said.

She was acting so nonchalant about Will's belongings that I didn't know how much longer I would be able to hold myself together. Will's possessions were all that he had left in this world, along with Sami. Of course, I wanted to have them. Money would not have been an issue for me to make sure that all of his things were properly handled. But Da Wife had sold his things, and probably at flea market prices. It took everything I had in me not to go off on her about that. Keeping my cool was harder with each passing second. The server appeared and started removing the used dishes and utensils from the table, which was just what I needed to get myself together.

"Will this be one or two checks?" the server asked with a friendly smile.

"You can make them separate," Da wife suggested.

"I'm glad we had the opportunity to meet and clear the air today, Robin. Thanks for meeting me," I said.

"It was good seeing you and having the opportunity to see you face to face to get my feelings off my chest," she acknowledged.

We both remained calm and casual, paid our tabs, and went our separate ways. I would never have the opportunity of collecting the box of things she said once belonged to Will because she would never give it to me.

Eli phoned me after leaving church to see if I was done with the brunch meeting.

"Hey babe, just checking on you to make sure you're good and that you didn't have to catch a case with Da Wife," he joked.

"Yes, I'm good. It went as well as to be expected considering there's no room for salvaging our friendship due to the hurt and my feelings of betrayal and lack of loyalty," I said truthfully.

"I'm sure a little retail therapy would lift your spirits. I'll run home to change then come by your place to pick you up. Then, you can go with me to Neiman Marcus to do some shopping for a coworker's last day tomorrow, and I'll buy you a nice pair of shoes," he offered.

"Hmmm, so you're not one of those guys that thinks if you purchase a man shoes he will walk out of your life?" I asked and giggled like a high school boy.

"Tyler, I don't believe in those superstitions as I don't believe in not purchasing you a watch because it will shorten our time together."

"That's good to hear. I agree totally with you," I said.

"Hell, I feel if I like something I want to see on you I am going to purchase it and enjoy it on you each time you wear it whether it be shoes, clothing, accessories or cologne," Eli said.

"Thanks for the gesture and offer. I really could use some retail therapy as a pick me upper. Be safe getting home to change. I'm heading back now to let Sami out to potty and poop and will await your arrival," I said ending the call.

Minutes later, I walked into my condo and grabbed Sami's leash.

"Come on, girl. Let's go for a quick walk around the bridge. Daddy's about to go out for some retail therapy," I said to Sami.

I called Bobbie once Sami and I started strolling the neighborhood.

Hey, babe," Bobbie said answering her mobile.

"Hello, love. What are you up to?" I asked.

"About to start that fight doing Maia's hair since you won't do it for me," she said in a sharp tone.

"I would, but Eli wants me to go with him shopping once he comes to pick me up."

"Well, in that case, I don't blame you. Throw me a sexy lingerie set in there and tell him it's for your girl." She laughed.

I boomed with loud laughter. "Let me see what I'm getting first before I start adding your laundry list of things, but I got you."

"How did the meeting with Da Wife go?" she asked, striking down my jovial mood with just one question.

"About as I expected. We talked about how she felt about me not being there for her after the miscarriage and how she had Will's things and got rid of them with the exception of a box of his things for me and a box for each parent." I sighed my disappointment, still in disbelief over Da Wife belittling my importance in Will's life to one single box.

"Wait a minute! You're telling me your so-called friend that married your husband tells you that she has a box of your man's things yet never called you to see how you wanted to handle or dispense the remainder of his things even things you two purchased together?" Bobbie grated out. The frustration in her tone matched my own.

"That's exactly right. It's all good though. I'll let what happens happen as I continue my healing. I've forgiven her and wish her well. Put Maia on the phone; I'd rather talk to her than put more energy into discussing Da Wife," I said.

"You're better than me," Bobbie said. "Hold on, here she is."

"Uncle Tyler, what you doing? Are you coming to see me?" Maia asked in her tiny, soft voice. My niece had a way of cheering me up with just hearing her say my name.

"I won't be able to this time, baby, but do Uncle Tyler a favor please," I asked.

"Okay. What is it?"

"When Mommy blow dries your hair and braids it, promise me to be a big girl and not cry for me. We will go to Chuck E Cheese next time I come pick you up, okay?" I pleaded, and low-key bribed her.

"Okay, Uncle Tyler." Maia's voice perked up.

"Thank you, my big girl. I love you."

"I love you too, Uncle Tyler."

"Give mommy back the phone, and I'll speak with you later."

"Mommy, Uncle Tyler wants to speak back with you," she said passing the phone to Bobbie.

"Sami, stop that barking. I can't hear," I yelled.

"You know your niece is looking at me like y'all been talking long enough, and I'm not about to listen to you and that yelping dog of yours, so I'm going to let you go and get ready. Tell Eli hello, and I look forward to meeting him," Bobbie rambled on.

"Look here now, you leave my barking dog alone and give Maia a kiss for me," I laughingly said.

"Love you, babe. Enjoy your day. Don't forget about a sister in the mall," she reminded me.

"Love you more, and I'll give Eli your message," I said ending the call.

Just as I walked through the door and took Sami's leash off to give her a treat and water, Eli rang my phone.

"Hello, sir," I answered.

"Hey there, I'm pulling up if you want to head on out," he said.

"Okay, coming out now."

I walked outside to Eli's car and reached for the door handle.

"Wait a minute," Eli said through the window. He hopped out the car and walked around to open the door for me. "Your chariot has arrived, sir," he said, opening the door.

"Thanks, Eli. Such a thoughtful gentleman, you are."

"Keep me around for another seven to eight months. There's more to come," he responded with a wink of his eye.

"I will say this is a great start to what is to come, and I'm feeling it and you." I leaned in to give him a kiss.

"Tyler, I know that we are both men, but I believe in chivalry. Please allow me the honor of opening the door for you when you're in my presence," Eli said with a pleading look in his brown eyes.

"It's a beautiful gesture that I welcome and receive, so sure thing, sir."

"Did you want to grab something to eat before we hit the stores or vice versa?" he asked.

"I'm still kind of stuffed from brunch. Unless you are feeling peckish, I can wait until we are done," I answered.

"I can wait. I'll just run into Starbuck's to get me a caramel macchiato. Then, we can be on our way. Let's find her gift first, and then we can look for ourselves and take our time," Eli suggested.

"Anything you'd like, Eli. I'm just glad to be spending the day with you and getting my mind off of my meeting earlier," I admitted.

"You know I'm all ears if you want to talk about it. I'm here for your support, baby," he said.

"We have so many more important things to talk about and look forward to. It's passed, she's the past, and Tyler is enjoying his time with Eli this beautiful Sunday," I said.

"Well Tyler, I like the sound of that. Just know whatever you need me to be or do, you have it," Eli said sincerely.

"Thanks, babe. Being right here in this moment is all I need. Oh, my friend Bobbie wanted me to tell you hello, and she can't wait to meet you."

"I look forward to meeting her as well," Eli said, pulling up to the mall. He parked the car, and I sat and waited for him to turn off the ignition and get out to open the door for me. "I saw this pendant from Tiffany's I'd like to get my coworker. We can head in there and purchase it, get it wrapped, and then head to Sak's for me to spoil you, sir," Eli said smiling.

I followed his lead, and soon we were entering Tiffany's.

"Welcome to Tiffany's," the greeter announced.

"Thank you, sir," we said in unison.

I walked over to the section where the sunglasses were to give Eli time with the sales clerk to purchase the gift for his coworker. I tried on a few pair of sunglasses and had just picked up another when Eli whispered in my ear.

"That second pair looked very nice on you." He stood behind me, so close that I could feel the heat from his words.

"How do you know? You were over there purchasing the gift," I said flirtatiously.

"As you tried each pair on, I was looking at you through the mirror adjacent to you. We should get them for you," he commanded.

"No, I'll get them another time."

Eli turned to the sales clerk. "Ma'am, I'd like to get those sunglasses on the second from the top shelf for him, please… as you settle my check."

"Someone is very lucky this evening. Is this a special occasion?" the clerk asked.

"Not at all. This thoughtful gentleman simply knows how to treat a fella," I answered.

"That I do," Eli said winking his eye at me. "Thanks for your help, Jackie. Have a great afternoon," Eli said to the clerk as we walked away.

"Let me grab the door, and thanks, kind sir," I said as we exited the store.

"You are more than welcome, Tyler. Thank you for allowing me to get them for you. Are you cool with us heading to Mezlan to look at some shoes before we go to Nordstrom and Saks'?"

"That's fine. There's a pair of shoes I've been looking at online. It would be nice if they're on sale, so I can purchase them," I said.

"If they have the pair in my size that I've wanted my last couple of visits, we will both walk out with our shoes," Eli said.

"Good afternoon gentleman. Welcome to Mezlan. Let me know if I can be of any assistance to you," the greeter said as we entered.

"Thank you, sir. We will let you know." I walked to the shoes I wanted.

"I love that shoe, Tyler. You won't believe this, but that is the shoe I've been wanting to get the past couple of months," Eli said admiring the shoe in my hand.

"Great minds think alike. You have good taste in shoes and, as far as I can see, in men too," I teased with a laugh.

"Pardon me. Could we try this shoe on in an eleven and a half and a ten?" Eli asked a nearby salesperson.

"Now, how did you know my shoe size, sir?" I asked with a raised eyebrow.

"I study feet and have worked in retail enough to pay attention to detail. As I scrolled through your pictures on Instagram, one of your pictures had the label of a twelve in your slides you had showing your feet." He nudged me. "Am I correct, sir?"

I nodded. The salesperson came toward us with three boxes, "I have sizes ten, eleven, and a twelve," he said.

"I'll make this size eleven work if the twelve is too large," I said clutching both boxes.

"You, sir, just be sure not to wear them the same time I'm wearing mine!" Eli scoffed.

"Noted," I replied.

"How do those work for you gentlemen?" the salesperson asked.

"Perfectly," we answered as one voice then looked at one another with a smile.

"Well, I will take them and meet you at the register unless you have any questions or would like to look at other selections," the salesperson said.

"Did you want to look at any other shoes, Tyler?" Eli asked.

"No, I'm good. Those are fine with me."

"That will be all, sir. We will meet you at the register," Eli told the salesperson.

"The shoe looked very good on you, Eli. Can't wait to see what you will wear with them," I said.

"Thanks, I will wear them with this suit I have sitting in my closet waiting on them to come home." Eli laughed.

"I can only imagine. I bet you have the pocket square and lapel pin set on ready," I said.

"And you know this, sir. Come on; let's get out of here so we can hit these other two stores. Then, we can go eat. I'm getting kind of hungry," he suggested.

"I hope that you guys found everything to your satisfaction. Please take my card in case you should ever need anything. I'm Kyle; how would you like me to close this purchase?" he asked.

"Thanks, Kyle, we did find everything we needed. You can place both pair on this card," Eli said, handing Kyle his credit card.

"Lunch or dinner is on me, and thanks again," I whispered in his ear, blowing my breath into his beautiful brown lobe at the same time. It was a turn on to be out with a man like Eli, and an even bigger one to have him do thoughtful things like open my car door and treat me to a gift. Those are the things chivalry is made of.

"You're welcome. And, if that's the case, let's go to Davio's," Eli suggested an expensive restaurant before roaring out in laughter.

"Davio's it is. Anything for the handsome man that shows chivalry," I said seriously.

"You gentleman have a great Sunday afternoon. I put my scheduled days on the back of the card should you need to come back," Kyle said.

"Our pleasure. Thanks, Kyle. You have a great afternoon, as well," I said, grabbing the bags from his outstretched hand.

"Do you want to go to Nordstrom's or Sak's first?" Eli asked as we exited the store.

"Babe, to be honest with you, we don't have to do either. You've purchased me a pair of sunglasses now shoes. I will not let you buy me another thing," I said.

"Tyler, let me do nice things for you. I want to shower you," he said.

"I'll tell you what. Let me take you to Davio's to eat, then we can decide if we're still up for shopping once we are done." I hoped he'd allow me to treat him before we continued shopping on his dime.

"Deal," he said after a long pause.

We walked towards the mall's restaurant. Upon entering, the greeter said, "Good afternoon, welcome to Davio's. How many will be in your party?"

"Afternoon, two please," I said.

"Follow me this way," he said.

"I'm going to run to the restroom and meet you at the table," Eli said, and I nodded and watched him stroll toward the illuminated bathroom signs.

"Bethany will be your server and will be with you shortly," the greeter announced, bringing my attention back to him.

"Oh, thank you," I said, sitting down at our table.

"You're welcome! Enjoy your meal," the greeter added.

"Whew, I thought I was going to wet my pants. My zipper got stuck," Eli said with a relieved look on his face.

"Glad you were able to unzip, sir. That would have really been a scene," I said, which caused us both to erupt into laughter.

"Tell me about it," Eli was saying when our waitress arrived at the table smiling to the high heavens.

"Welcome to Davio's. My name is Bethany, and I'll be taking care of you today. What drink can I start you off with?" she asked in a cheerful tone. From her mood alone, my day was getting better.

"I think we are ready to order, are we Tyler?" Eli asked.

"Sure," I answered.

"I will start with you then, sir," Bethany said to Eli.

"I will have water with lime, the penne, applewood smoked chicken, sundried tomatoes, walnuts and cream and a glass of your house wine with my meal," Eli ordered.

"And you sir?" she asked.

"I will have water with lime as well, and for my entrée, your seared Atlantic salmon, baby spinach, warm eggplant caponata, and we will have your calamari as a starter," I said before asking, "Bethany, have you been told you have a strong resemblance to Kate Beckinsale?"

"Thank you. That's a huge compliment! I think she's beautiful, but yes, I have heard that on a few occasions. I'll get your order into the kitchen and be right back with your drinks."

We thanked Bethany, and she walked away.

"I hope she likes her gift and that the few coworkers that didn't contribute their money do so tomorrow," Eli said.

"Me too, and you know that you could never go wrong with Tiffany's."

"I guess you're right. I have a question for you, Tyler."

"Yes, sir. Ask away."

"How do you feel about exclusivity, about marriage?" he asked.

"To answer the first part, I must say it's important to me as I'm very selfish and greedy when it comes to my mate. And as for marriage, I long to marry the man I'd like to spend the rest of my life with," I answered, thinking back to Will and what we once shared.

"If this doesn't sound judgmental, why didn't you and your late partner marry?" he asked as lines of curiosity etched his forehead.

"It's kind of complicated," I answered.

"We've got time as we are waiting on our drinks and meal." He chuckled.

"There are two reasons why we didn't get a chance to marry. I will discuss one reason today and will share reason number two at a later time, deal?" I asked.

"I am all ears, Tyler, and if at any time you feel uncomfortable and want to change the subject, I am fine with that too. I just want to get to know this handsome gentleman sitting across from me a little more," he said.

"Thanks. You know I met with Robin earlier, right?"

"Yes, she's the one you referred to as Da Wife?" he replied.

"That is correct. Will decided years ago to marry someone so that he could have the pleasure of having a home off base and that Sami and I could be with him. He first asked my friend, Lady T, to marry him, but she declined as she hoped the guy she was dating would eventually marry her," I divulged.

"Just to make sure I am understanding you correctly before you move forward, your late partner Will was married to your friend Robin or as you refer to her Da Wife?" he asked.

"That is correct. It was an arranged marriage that we all three agreed upon. The night before he died due to hypertension and heart failure, he proposed to me and said, 'Tyler, move here with me, and I will divorce Robin so that you and I can wed.' But he died later in that night," I explained.

"I get it now. Thanks for opening up and sharing with me. Is that all of the one reason you wanted to share, or is there more, since you want to discuss reason number two at a later time?" he asked.

"Applewood smoked chicken?" the greeter said arriving at our table. We were so engrossed in our conversation that we didn't see her coming.

"That would be me," Eli answered with a partially raised hand.

"And here's your seared Atlantic salmon. Enjoy your lunch," he said as he walked away.

"Saved by the server," I said with a soft giggle.

"You don't have to share any more than you'd like, Tyler. I'm sure it's still hard on you," he said.

"Thanks, Eli. Let us bless the food." I reached for his hands.

"Good idea. I'm almost at starving level," he smirked.

"Dear Creator of the Universe, we thank you for allowing us to see another day and a day of fellowship with one another. Bless the food that we are about to partake and the hands that prepared it. Please continue to be our guide as we open up to one another and take this journey of getting to know one another. These and all blessings we ask, and in your son's name, we pray. Amen."

"Amen," Eli chimed and began carving his meat. "This chicken is so tender and moist. Would you like to try some?"

"It does look delicious, but having bacon laying across it, I have to decline. Thanks for the offer. This salmon is seared to perfection though. You should try it, so when you have me over for dinner, you'll know the consistency I'd like," I joked, extending my fork to him.

"Very funny but noted." He opened his mouth as I fed him. "Since you've just shared an intimate and deep part of your life with me, I'll open up some to you," Eli said.

"I'm all ears." I took a bite of my eggplant caponata.

"As a little boy, pleasing my father was the most important thing to me. I wanted him to love me, be proud of me, and simply see me," Eli began. "I tried to do all things that boys do, so he wouldn't call or think of me as a sissy or anything."

"I never had the opportunity to grow up with a father, as mine was murdered just a couple days after my birth. I cannot imagine the thought of having to please one," I interjected.

"With the trying to fight my sexuality and please not only my father but society and my family, I dated a girl that got pregnant and could possibly have a daughter out there," he sighed.

I reached to touch his hand. "Wow. Do you know where the mother and possible daughter is, and how's your relationship with your father now?"

"Pops and my relationship have gotten stronger over the years; we are almost like best friends. As for who could possibly be my daughter, I have an idea of where she and her mother live, but when I last contacted her mother and asked was it my child she told me no," Eli said.

"Glad to know you and your father have a great relationship. Wish that was my fate. As for your potential daughter, if you have a gut feeling and want to be a part of her life, then request a paternity test to see," I said encouragingly.

"Thanks, man. Pops really a cool guy. You would like him, and I'll have you meet him one day soon. I hate that you never got a chance to meet your father; my condolences to you." Eli stood up from the booth and came to my side of the table. He kneeled to hug me, placing my head on his shoulder as he stroked my back in a caring way.

"God makes no mistakes. My life would probably be so different had he been around," I said.

"You're right. As for the paternity test, I'll think about it. Wouldn't want to go in and disrupt her life after she's been on this earth for seventeen years either thinking someone else is her father or simply not knowing," Eli said pensively.

"That's a valid point. You asked me about marriage and exclusivity; how do you feel about them?" I asked.

"Exclusivity, I am a one man's man, but I do love to flirt and am somewhat an attention seeker. With that being said, I would never step out of my relationship to disrespect my partner," he said.

"Hmmmmm," I replied.

"Marriage, I do want to be married but not really sure if the man I want to marry exists unless he could possibly be sitting across from me," he suggested.

"What are the odds of that man being across from you right now? What traits do I possess that you've seen so far that would make you think I am him?" I asked.

"First, I will say that you're very considerate of others. I've watched how you engage with people like when we were on our first date at Einstein's, when we were at Tiffany's and Mezlan, and even here. Such a courteous dude. How you are willing to open up to me and show interest in what's going on in my world plus making suggestions to make it better," he said with a slight twinkle in his eye.

I smiled.

"Thanks, Eli. I try to be respectful and courteous to mankind. I'm in a service providing industry, so I get it how people are always trying to make certain of client satisfaction. I guess I got that from my late grandmother; believing in what goes around comes back around," I reasoned.

"I admire that you're a go-getter with that hustler, boss mentality. You're very easy on the eye with that sexy, distinguished look," Eli doted me with compliments.

"I appreciate that, kind sir. I try. Watching my mother work hard to raise and support eight kids with the help of my grandmother made me strive to be and do more," I said.

"If you could have a perfect day, what would that day look like for you, Tyler?" Eli asked.

Great question.

"I'm already having it," I answered.

"If it could be out of the norm, please share," he pressed.

"To wake up in a bungalow on the water in Maldives or Bora Bora with the wind blowing and drapes whistling to the sound of the breeze while smelling the aroma of blueberry muffins or pancakes and turkey bacon coming from an adjacent bungalow with a kitchenette," I said.

"I can visualize this. Tell me more," Eli said with a glimmer in his eyes as if he were already in the Maldives experiencing it.

"Crawl out of bed and put a tank and shorts on my naked body before going into the kitchen to have breakfast with my man before we start our day," I continued.

"So, where would your man be all of this time?" Eli asked.

"As I wake, he would be laying on his stomach and I on his back with my leg wrapped around his until I slowly move to wake him from his sleep."

"Hmmm, tell me more!" Eli yelped.

"I'd give him a kiss on his cheek then suggest to him that we get up and go have breakfast before our nice morning yoga on the pier for about thirty minutes," I added.

"Now that your man is out of bed?" he asked.

"He'd meet me in the lavatory to wash our faces and brush our teeth before heading into the breakfast nook for breakfast, while our server prepares our plates of the breakfast we were awakened to. And as she is pouring my freshly squeezed orange juice, she follows up with pouring him a cup of coffee to go along with our meals before we head out for our morning yoga and meditation." As I envisioned this fantasy moment, I was sure I had a glimmer in my eyes, as well.

"You shared with me that on this perfect day you've thrown on some shorts and a tank. What is your man wearing while you two are having breakfast?" he asked, appearing engulfed in my fantasy right along with me.

"He has on a pair of slides or sandals, as he knows that no socks are allowed in my presence, a pair of sheer lounge pants, and a fitted V-neck shirt," I answered.

"Oh, so you have a foot fetish I'm assuming?" Eli retorted.

"Yes, I do. May sound a bit shallow, but my dude has to have nice feet, teeth, hands, and an added bonus would be him having nice calves," I said.

"I have a question for you after you finish your perfect day," Eli said.

"Go ahead and ask now. I can resume my perfect day after your question," I insisted.

"So, if I, or a guy that shows you interest, do not have nice feet, hands, teeth or even nice calves, they don't stand a chance with you?" he asked.

"I'm not saying that it's a deal breaker, but those nice features are a plus as I love a beautiful smile, smooth, manicured hands with groomed feet and perfectly formed calves that I can run my feet against during spooning or cuddling. It makes it a great night's rest for me," I said, laughing as I revealed my desires.

"Guess it's a good thing I keep these claws and paws done, genetically blessed with nice calves, and wore braces two times around," Eli said with a loud chuckle.

"Yes, sir and that deep, baritone voice is a plus too," I said with a wink. The vibrations of his voice raked through me every time he opened his mouth to speak, which was what made talking to him so intriguing.

"Alright now, let's get back to your perfect day," Eli said with a bit of wonderment in his tone.

I smiled, eager to continue the journey we were taking together.

"So, I left off telling you what he'd be wearing. He will have on some lounge pants, fitted V-neck shirt and slides or sandals while we are having breakfast. Then, we go into the room to put on our compressors and tanks. We'd walk out on the pier while the sun is beaming on our face and the sounds of wind blowing while listening to the Patrick O'Hearn Pandora Station."

"What will you guys do after yoga and meditation?" Eli asked.

"We will then take a nice, hot shower together, and I'll call for a couples' massage on our private patio. Then, we would have a late lunch, maybe go jet skiing, parasailing or water skiing," I added.

"Then?"

"Do some tourist things and go back to the bungalow to freshen up and get dressed for dinner and dancing," I said.

"What would you wear, and would you dress him?" he asked.

"I'd have him wear a pair of linen pants, sandals, and a tank to show off his physique. I would wear a romper and a mule fitted just enough to entice him to desire me the entire time we are out for dinner and on the dance floor, with hopes he can't keep his hands off of me until we get back to the bed for the night," I suggested seductively.

"I've heard about enough because now you have my bird growing, and I'm becoming very hormonal at the moment," Eli said.

"How are you two enjoying your meals?" Bethany interrupted with seemingly perfect timing.

"Everything is great. Thanks, and you can bring the check, please," I said.

"Will this be one or two checks?" she asked.

"One please and thanks," I answered.

"I could use a nap right now. Do you think we could lay down together and just cuddle a bit; I promise not to do anything?" Eli asked.

"Yes, we probably could but being that you've already suggested you're hormonal, I don't think it would be easy for you to just lay in bed beside me and rest peacefully," I answered.

"Come on, Tyler. Let's at least give it a try. It will be simply one of many times that are to come of me holding you while snoring in your ear and squeezing you tight as we slumber," he enticed me with the idea of being wrapped up in his arms.

"I will allow an early pass since you've been so good to me today, taking me shopping and getting my mind off of my visit with Da Wife today, but on one condition," I halted.

"Anything, Tyler," he muttered.

"We will lay on the sofa, and I'll use a throw to cover us up, you on the outside while I hold you," I offered.

"That's a deal I can't refuse. I promise to be on my best behavior," Eli said just as the check came.

We made it to my condo about twenty-five minutes later, and Eli said, "Babe, I'll take Sami for a walk. You get the cover and find something for us to watch and be waiting for me to nestle under you."

"Thanks for that. I'll do just that!" I responded and grabbed some covers and put on something more comfortable.

"She must've been waiting on this because she went out and pooped immediately and pissed twice," he said as he entered the door after their quick walk.

"My baby just wanted to get back in and get her a treat. Isn't that right, Sami?" I asked, rubbing my pooch between the ears.

"I'm going to use the bathroom and remove my clothes. Did you find us a movie?" Eli asked.

"Let me put food down and freshen her water. Then, I'll look for something" I answered

"I will find us something. Just finish taking care of Sami," he said, looking through the DVDs.

"Sounds like a plan," I said, and within minutes, I joined Eli in the living room. "She's all taken care of. Now, let me hold my five-nine, cuddly bear," I joked.

"Hey, what's up with this DVD that says Tyler's fortieth birthday?" he inquired.

"It is what it says, you genius, Tyler's fortieth birthday!" I shrugged as I laughed.

"Lay down. I'll insert it. Let me see the man I'm falling in love with." Eli smiled.

"You might see me in a different light." I laughed and put my arms around him as he settled on the sofa.

After twenty-nine minutes of watching my birthday video, he turned on his back and looked me in the eyes. "Tyler, do you think your family and friends will suggest you're dating me because I remind you of Will?" he asked.

"I don't see why they would suggest or think that because you don't remind me of Will," I answered.

"Well, I can see some resemblance after looking at him in your video," he said.

Laying there looking at the ceiling, I questioned myself. *Is that reason I'm so into him because there's some resemblance of Will, or is it because he cares for and treats me like Will treated me?*

"Hey, you okay?" Eli asked.

"Yes, just thought about Will, and a letter I need to complete that I started a few days ago. That's all," I said in a low tone.

Eli reached down and pecked my cheek.

"If you ever need to talk about anything, I'm here for you, Tyler," he said then slid from the sofa and ejected the DVD from the machine. He found another movie for us to watch, *The Best Man Holiday,* and we spent the next two hours in relative silence, just enjoying each other's nearness and companionship.

CHAPTER EIGHT

SEX WITH ME

After a year of dating, I suggested Eli move in with me since he was practically at my place all the time. It was more convenient for him to get to work, and his roommate seemed to not want Eli there anymore.

"Hey babe, how's the packing going?" I asked him.

"Just have to load three more boxes into the car, then I will head over to put some things into my storage before heading to your place," Eli said.

"Be careful and let me know when you're near. I will meet you in the alley with your key and key fob to get into the parking garage," I said.

"I can't say enough how much I appreciate you, Tyler. I'm one lucky guy and blessed to have you as my boyfriend."

"I feel you, babe. I love you, Eli," I said ending our call. The next morning, Eli and I were curled underneath the covers when my alarm rang out. "Morning Babe, it's 5 a.m. Time to get up; we are going to be late for the gym," I said against his ear.

"Five more minutes, please," Eli whined.

"Come on get up. I told you to bring your butt to bed last night. You know AJ is going to have us running laps if we are late, so get up!" I yelled.

"Alright…alright, will you fix me a shake as I wash my face and brush my teeth?" he asked.

Most mornings, Eli would prepare our lunch while I'd get our clothes together before showering. Oftentimes, I would drop him off at work before going to work and picking him up on some days to keep him from having to drive. Our relationship was magical. Not only did Eli try to give me everything my heart desired, but he was such a big supporter of everything that was important to me from marketing the salon to book sales and my scholarship foundation. He introduced me to his circle of friends as I introduced him to mine and my family.

"It's already done and on the counter. I'm going to get the car," I said.

"Okay, I'll be out in a moment," he said.

"Did you grab your gloves off the bar stool?" I asked when he arrived at the car looking groggy.

"Thanks for the shake, baby, and yes I have them. May I have a kiss?" he asked.

"Muah," I blew him an air kiss.

"If we are late, I will tell AJ it's my fault and to have me run the laps alone," Eli said.

"Deal."

We pulled up at AJ Mastin Fitness, and the parking lot was full. From the looks of it, the class had started.

"Good morning, all," I said, entering the room.

"You guys know what time it is," AJ said.

"AJ, it's all my fault. Let Tyler jump in, and I'll do the laps myself," Eli pleaded his case for me.

"Tyler, jump in; you get a pass today," AJ said.

After our hour group fitness workout, we headed home to get ready for work. I entered the shower as soon as we got home. Moments later, Eli yelled, "Tyler your cell is ringing!"

"Who is it?"

"Lady T."

"I'll answer it from the shower, thanks," I said. "Hello."

"Hey baby; how are you?" Lady T asked.

"I'm good, just in from the gym and in the shower getting ready for work. What do I owe the pleasure of this call so early in the morning?" I asked.

"I won't hold you, but let's go dancing tonight," she said giddily.

"Cool, let me get out of this shower and call you back, and we can discuss it more," I said.

"No need. Get yourself ready, and I'll shoot you the location and time via text. Have a productive day, and see you tonight," she spat out, leaving me no room to decline.

"Alright, love you." I ended the call to accept another call waiting from my friend in Texas.

"Hello, Stacia!" I said with excitement to hear from her.

"Good morning, handsome. Sorry to call so early, but do you have a quick moment?" Stacia asked.

"Sure, I was about to jump in the shower, but it can wait. What's going on?" I asked, beaming with curiosity.

"Harris and I have set a date, and it will be a very small wedding ceremony of important people in our lives. I would love for you and Eli to attend and, of course, have you do my hair!" she exclaimed.

"Of course, we will be in attendance, and I'd love to do your hair. I'll call Lacey to do your makeup so we can tag team you for your special day," I suggested.

"That would be awesome. I wanted to get that confirmed before your invitation arrives in a day or two," she said.

"Knock, knock," Eli said as he tapped against the bathroom door. "Clothes are on the bed."

"Hold up, babe. I have Stacia on speaker, and she's inviting you and me to attend her wedding."

"Good morning, Stacia. Nothing would give us greater pleasure than witnessing your union to Harris. Tell him congratulations and same to you. I've gotta run. Nice chatting with you!" Eli said as he was about to close the door.

"Stacia, hold on for a second." I placed her on mute.

"Babe, did you leave your sweaty socks for me?" I asked, knowing I liked to sniff his socks.

"Ewwww, and yes, right where you told me to leave them," he said.

"Thanks. You are too kind." I chuckled.

"I'm going to drive today because some coworkers and I are going out after work," he said.

"Sounds like fun. Lady T wants me to go out with her tonight."

"Where are you all going?" he asked.

"Not sure; she said she would text me location and time," I replied.

"Be safe going to work, and have a productive day. I'll see you later tonight," he said as I walked out of the bathroom.

"Kisses, you do the same," I said and unmuted the call. "Stacia, I'm back. Sorry for the long hold."

"No worries, I know you have to get ready for your day, and I have a million more things to do. I love you, handsome. Have a great weekend. Kisses," she said as we ended the call.

** * **

After my last client, I received that text from Lady T saying we'd go check out this lounge called Soundtable. I dashed home to shower and met her at the lounge. She was valeting her car when I pulled up. Lady T was wearing a canary yellow halter top with some nicely fitted white linen pants and a pair of red Adrienne Vittadini sandals.

"You look so sexy tonight, lady," I said leaning down to give her a hug.

"As always, you look sexy, Tyler. I love these fitted jeans and this asymmetrical tank you're wearing," she said.

As we entered the club, she was really feeling herself from the compliments of her newly inverted haircut I'd just given her a month ago. We approached the bar and waited to be served. At the other end of the bar, I noticed an attractive couple that nodded and waved at us.

"I'll have a Blue Hawaii," I said to the bartender.

Lady T ordered her favorite. "A glass of Zinfandel, please," she said.

The bartender left us to prepare our drinks and when he returned said, "The couple at the other end of the bar took care of your drinks."

We raised our glasses with a cheer, and I pulled her to the dance floor when the sounds of Bruno Mars' "24K Magic" exploded through the speakers. We were gyrating our hips and feeling the music as the disc jockey rolled over to "Rock With U" by Janet Jackson. He turned on the strobe lights, and the energy in the building was electrifying. We were in disco heaven before we realized the couple from the bar was dancing on us. The female had grabbed Lady T's waist and pulled her in closer to her.

"I love your haircut and your outfit," she said to Lady T.

The guy was grinding close enough against me for me to feel his erection. He leaned over to whisper in my ear, "Do you want to do with me what the song is saying?" he asked as Rhianna's "Sex with Me" came on.

I felt uncomfortable when I noticed a familiar face sitting at the bar lurking at me; it was Sinclair, the guy I met walking Sami one morning. We had spoken a few times over the phone, but I didn't give it much thought since Eli and I were exclusive and living together. I could sense Sinclair wasn't feeling the strange man grinding on me.

"Excuse me," I said leaving the dance floor to go to the men's restroom.

Then, the six foot six lean, Adonis started dancing with Lady T and his lady.

As soon as I entered the restroom, Sinclair came in, grabbed me and pulled me into a stall. He started kissing me, pulling up my shirt, and talking shit.

"No other man should be touching you like that," he whispered then proceeded to bury his tongue down my throat as I pushed him off of me. "Why are you resisting me, and why haven't you called me back?" he asked. He reached down to put my hand on his erection and started squeezing my hand then biting on my earlobe. "You know you want me. Stop fighting it, Tyler."

"I can't, Sinclair. I'm seeing someone now."

He pushed me away. "Is that why you haven't called me back lately?"

"I didn't really think you were interested. You never asked me out on a date, and I only hear from you ever so often," I admitted.

"My job requires me to travel a lot. I'm living in two different states," he said.

"Does your phone not work between your travel? I'm just asking because we make time for what we want," I said.

"You got me on that. You're a very sexy dude, Tyler. I really want to get to know you. I have been dealing with a lot at work and helping a good friend out that relocated here. I apologize for not making you a priority."

"No worries; it's all good," I assured him.

"But it's no coincidence with we keep meeting like this," he said.

"I really need to get back out there because that couple was all over my girl and me. Need to make sure she's fine," I said.

"I will go with you!" he said trailing behind me.

I reached Lady T and pulled her over to the side of the dance floor. "I think I'm about to leave and head home. Are you going to stay here?" I asked.

"You think you're slick. You're not about to head home. Where are you and that guy going?" she asked, pointing at Sinclair.

"I don't know where he's going, but I'm really heading home," I said.

"If you say so, Tyler. I'm staying here. After we leave here, I'm meeting them at a house party somewhere in Buckhead," she said, pointing at the couple that we met at the bar.

"Please be safe, and text me the address when you get there. Let me know that you're alright," I pleaded.

"Okay, but excuse me, hello sir," Lady T said to Sinclair. "I'm Lady T, and I'm not sure what your intentions are with my baby, but you'd better not hurt him!"

"Hello, Lady T. Nice to meet you. I'm Sinclair, and I simply wanted to take your friend out on a date, but he shares with me that's he's already spoken for, so you have no worries. I won't say that I'm going to stop pursuing him, but I will respect his relationship," Sinclair said.

"I'm serious T. Send me the address and assure me you are okay. Do not, and I repeat, do not under any circumstance get in the car with them!" I demanded.

"I hear you. I will be safe. You get home safely. Kisses," she said heading back to the dance floor to join the couple. The man looked disappointed when he saw me walk away with Sinclair.

At the valet, awaiting our cars, Sinclair asked, "Is it possible for us to have a platonic date just to meet for coffee or tea?"

"I can't say that would be a good idea. There's some attraction between us, not to mention what just happened in the men's restroom a moment ago," I said.

"Consider this then. If your beau fucks up, give me a call," he said with a raised eyebrow.

"Deal." I shook his hand, and the valet driver pulled up in a burgundy Aston Martin and left the door opened for Sinclair.

"Well, this is me. It was so good seeing you, Tyler. I hope to hear from you soon, and please get home safely," he said.

"I will, and you do the same. Nice car."

"Thanks. Don't be a stranger, Tyler. Good night." Sinclair pulled off, leaving me standing on the curb watching him leave out of my view.

"Here's your car, sir. Have a good night." The valet snapped me out of the daze of what could have been if I weren't already a taken man. I really didn't feel like going home, and the night was still young, so I decided to go to Whiskey Mistress.

As I pulled up, the valet opened the door for me to exit the car. I walked inside and, wouldn't you know, Peaches was on the mic singing "Did You Ever Love Me" by Deborah Cox. Her voice sent chills down my spine. I waved at Peaches after her performance, and she made her way over to me. "Hey, Tyler. How are you doing?" she asked.

"All is well. Thanks for asking, and you?"

"No complaints, Tyler."

"That was one of my favorite songs by Deborah."

"I love her, too. I hope you enjoyed it," she said.

"I did. Are you performing anymore tonight?" I asked.

"No, I'm going to head on out of here. I need to get to bed early. I am driving down to Savannah tomorrow morning," she said.

"What's in Savannah?" I asked.

"One of my friends told me they need a stand-in tomorrow at Casimir's lounge. The singer that normally performs had a family emergency, and they're willing to pay me fifteen hundred dollars to only sing two songs," she said.

"Not sure what the going rate is, but that sounds like that's worth the drive," I said.

"It is. I've never been to Savannah so this will be exciting. Only thing is I'll be locked in my hotel room until it's time to perform since I don't know anyone there," she said.

"Savannah is a beautiful place. There will be a lot for you to do. I've been a few times." I said.

"Why don't you come along with me and be my companion and tour guide? I'll take care of your lodging since they are taking care of mine and your meals too," she offered.

"Now that sounds like an offer I can't refuse, and it gives me an opportunity to release a letter I just wrote for some needed closure," I said.

"Awesome, text me your address, and I'll pick you up tomorrow around nine a.m. I'm going to head on home and get some rest. You be safe driving home," Peaches said.

"I'm right behind you. I was only here to support and hear you, and it looks like I'll be getting that tomorrow." I walked out with her to wait on the valet to bring my car.

As I slid behind the wheel, a text came through from Lady T, letting me know the address to the party and that she felt safe.

The next morning around 9 a.m., Peaches picked me up in her beautiful red Jaguar to head to Savannah.

"I so love this car. The new leather smell and everything. Hmmm." I inhaled the aroma with closed eyes.

"I want you to lay back, relax and let the wind blow through your hair and face as Ms. Peaches jet sets us to Savannah. I was thinking we could go to Tybee Island while we are there," she said.

"Love the sound of that," I replied.

"Your phone is flashing," she said.

"Oh, that's Lady T." I answered the phone, "Hello, hot mama! What are you up to?"

"I wanted to see if you wanted to ride to see my son, and maybe we could stop over in Savannah for a few hours and grab a bite to eat and go to Tybee Island," Lady T offered.

"Funny you'd offer that. I'm in the car with Peaches heading to Savannah now. She's performing at a lounge there tonight," I said.

"Tell Peaches 'good morning.' Where are you all staying?" she asked.

"Peaches, T says 'good morning' and wants to know where we are staying?" I asked.

"Morning Lady T. We are staying at the Hotel Indigo. I hope you can come to support me tonight at the Casimir's Lounge," Peaches yelled into the phone.

"I will be there, Peaches," Lady T said. "You guys be careful, and I'll hit you up when I get there, Tyler. Love you," she added.

Three and a half hours later, we arrive at the hotel.

"Welcome to Hotel Indigo," the clerk said.

"Reservations for Peaches Davenport," Peaches stated.

"Ms. Davenport, I have your reservations for two rooms, is that correct?" the clerk asked.

"Yes, that's correct. Thank you," Peaches answered as her cell started ringing. "Hello Sin," she answered, putting the phone on speaker.

"Hey, beautiful. Just checking to see if you made it to Savannah safely?" Sin asked.

"Yes, I did thanks. A friend of mine rode down with me, and we are checking into our room now," she answered.

"Tell your friend thanks, and you should check out Paula Deen's restaurant while you're there. I wish I didn't have to go to Florida to check on my mother. I would have loved to come to support you tonight. Knock their socks off," Sin encouraged.

"Let me get checked in. Tell your parents hello for me, and safe travels," Peaches said.

As I sat there listening but not listening, her friend Sin sure sounded a lot like Sinclair, but what are the odds of that? I let the thought roll off my mind as the clerk began speaking.

"Ms. Davenport, I placed you and your guest in adjacent rooms 706 and 708 on the seventh floor. Let us know if you need anything, and enjoy your stay here in Savannah," she said.

"Thank you, and we will. Tyler, let's head up to drop our bags off then go grab lunch."

"You must hear my stomach growling? I'm getting a little peckish," I said then laughed.

"My friend, Sin, thanks you for riding with me and suggested we go to Paula Deen's restaurant while we are here."

"It's pretty good. Eli and I came two months ago," I said.

"Good. Well, text Lady T the address to the hotel and tell her we are on our way to lunch," Peaches said.

"Already done."

"You waste no time, sir," she said, laughing.

After we had finished lunch, Lady T met us at the hotel. Peaches had to run to the lounge for sound check, so Lady T and I headed over to Tybee Island, and Peaches would join us later.

"Lady T, you know I never got any real closure after Will's death. So, I wrote this letter to him, and I think I want to release it into the water so that I can release him to fully transition. This will give me an opportunity to be as one with Eli," I said.

"Tyler, Will loved him some you. I would sit and watch how he looked at you, sometimes. With my own eyes, I saw that you were the only guy in the world to him, and your love for him will never die," Lady T said, holding my hand tightly with water-filled eyes.

"I know. Even when we got on one another's nerve, we were still in love. I miss him so much, T," I said as a tear threatened to run down my cheeks. "Why did he have to leave so soon?"

"I don't know, Tyler. I miss him too, but he's always with you, right here," she said touching my heart. We walked up to the sand, approaching the water, and I pulled the letter out of my pocket. "I'm going to give you a moment to be alone, Tyler. I will just walk up ahead. Take your time… all the time you need."

Lady T walked away, and I walked along the beach as the cool water hit my ankles, my feet buried in the sand. The sound of seagulls ringing in my ear was a reminder as I looked over the letter that this may be my last time writing to my beloved, late partner. The tears rolled down my face as I read each word, and the sun shined brightly drying them up before they could reach my chin.

Will,

This has got to be the hardest thing I've had to endure since your passing…

You, sir, have made it very hard for me to let go, move on or forget you. I can't thank you enough for eleven years of love, growth, hurt, laughter, joy, etc. I could go on and on about my different emotions, but I'm sure you can feel my heart and know how much I love you, what you mean to me and how much I miss you. Although this is a tough thing for me to do, I feel in my heart that it's time I let you go, not only for me but for US… you need to make your transition onto the other side without having to continuously check in on me to make sure I'm okay; know that in time I will be. I need to release you so that some fortunate individual will have the experience of sharing the love from me that you once had.

You will always be in the upper chamber of my heart tucked safely away, as I will carry you every day. You will NEVER be forgotten. I will continue to campaign our love story as well as your legacy through the scholarship foundation I created on your behalf. I know that you are in great care in the company of your grandmother, my grandmother, my mother, B, and my sister. Give them all my love. Be free as I let you go to live my life without your physical being. I love you always and forever.

Tyler

I tossed the letter into the water and slowly walked to catch up with Lady T who was now accompanied by Peaches.

"Babe, are you alright?" Lady T asked.

"This can't be easy having closure with Will," Peaches interjected.

"Come here, I know it's hard, but know that you have so many people around you that love you with every breath of our being," Lady T said squeezing me tight.

"I want in," Peaches said.

"You're so silly; thanks, you all. I needed this."

"That's what friends are for," Peaches said.

"How did sound check go?" I asked her.

"It was great thanks. I'm actually going to head back to the room, so I can lay down and rest a bit. Then, I'll get up to have me a cup of tea before my performance tonight," Peaches said.

"I could actually do the same thing if you're ready to head on back, too," Lady T said.

"Lady T, you can stay in my room," I told her.

"Or, you can come in my room," Peaches offered. "You're definitely not wasting money on another room."

"I'll stay with Tyler, so he won't be alone," Lady T said with a genuine smile.

"That's a good idea. Maybe an hour before I'm to leave I want you two to help me decide what to wear tonight," Peaches asked, and three hours later we were knocking on her door, so we could help her decide what to wear for the show. She came around the corner in a knee-length Vince Camuto cutout sleeve, solid black dress and a pair of Vince Camuto court heel red sandals.

"You look absolutely stunning! I don't need to see another outfit. This is the one!" I screamed.

"I'm sorry, but I echo Tyler's input. Don't change a thing," Lady T said.

"Alright then. I'm going to head on over and start warming up with the band. I'll have your table reserved right in front of the stage," Peaches said before leaving, and T and I headed back to my room.

"What are you wearing, sexy man?" Lady T asked.

"My ripped skinny jeans and symmetrical fitted shirt with a zipper across the shoulder blade and my black Magnanni loafers," I answered.

"Well, tell me what you think of this romper I bought with me," she asked.

"That's cute, and a pretty shade of pink. What kind and color are your shoes?" I asked.

"This taupe Tory Burch sandal, you like?"

"Looks great. Now let's hurry and get dressed."

We got dressed and walked to the car. Once inside, Lady T proceeded to tell me about the couple from last night. "So, they led me to a house party where there was a lot of alcohol, drugs, and paraphernalia on the table. I knew it could get ugly. It wasn't something I wanted to be exposed to," she said, which had been my gut feeling about that couple.

"What did you do?" I asked.

"The chic was really feeling me, but I didn't know she was feeling me in a sexual kind of way until we got back to their place. She called herself Ms. J," Lady T said.

"So, where was the husband?" I asked.

"He asked me to take her home and hang out a bit with her and said he would be home shortly since I couldn't hang with the big boys," Lady T said. "He laughed it off, but I could tell he was upset."

"Interesting," I said.

"I didn't know whether to run for the hills or see what the night had in store for me," Lady T said.

"But your ass went, huh?" I laughed.

"When we got to the house, she started removing my strapless chocolate top and ivory palazzo pants, and I kicked off my sandals as we were entering the door. She throws me against the wall, starts kissing me, pulling gently on my hair as she's untying the halter top," she said.

"Wow, I'm getting kind of hot!" I joked.

"Before I knew it, she had me on the kitchen island with my legs in the air performing oral sex on me, licking my little flower endlessly and uncontrollably for what seemed like hours."

"I need a drink!" I gasped.

"It was an experience I could have never imagined, a woman giving me such pleasure that I had an orgasm three times back to back. As she stood up to go to the fridge to get some kiwi and grapes to lay on my little flower to eat them off, the garage door sounded, and the door leading to the kitchen opened. Her husband walked in on us."

"Hot! Then?" I asked.

"He approached the island as I lay vulnerable and naked and began lifting his shirt above his head to reveal his nicely sculpted twelve pack with both nipples pierced. He leaned in to kiss me as Ms. J strategically placed the kiwi and red grapes along my torso and nicely sugared crotch. He then unfastened his jeans and allowed them to drop to the floor revealing his ten-inch throbbing dick, and I could see it throbbing. He pushed Ms. J down to her knees to force her to give him oral pleasure as he buried his tongue deep in the walls of my little flower causing me to cum all over his face as he swallowed it and was being deep throated by his wife at the same time. When he licked me dry, he left me laying on the island drained and limp. He picked Ms. J up by the waist and carried her to the counter, pulled her to the edge, and fucked her uncontrollably until they climaxed," she said.

"Girl, I'm turned on. What happened next?" I asked, readjusting my pants.

"He said he was going to take a shower. Then, a little bit later, he came to the kitchen and carried each of us, one at a time, back to the shower and washed us down with a loofa. He dried us off before putting us into the bed. Then, he crawled in between us. He held me while she held him as we slept over into the next morning."

"I'm speechless. That is definitely an interesting night you had," I said.

"Yes, it was heavenly. Well, that's off my bucket list." She giggled.

"Whew, chile. Let's go in and hear Peaches blow," I said, grabbing her hand.

CHAPTER NINE

DID YOU EVER LOVE ME?

Sinclair Tate was born into a prestigious family in Barbados. Immediately after finishing high school, he decided to move to the states and get his degree in law. He received his undergraduate at Florida A & M, then later completed his degree in law at Seattle University School of Law. He made senior partner with the largest firm in Seattle, The Von Maur Law Group, in the heart of downtown. His life appeared to be perfect looking from the outside. He had a beautiful two and a half million dollar, five-bedroom, four-bathroom, three-car-garage home with the entire master bedroom facing the lake with glass from ceiling to floor. He wore the finest suits from Hickey Freeman, Hugo Boss to Zegna, and the shoes from Magnanni, Mezlan to Manolo Blahnik. Sinclair visited a different country once a month and handled cases in Atlanta once every other month at Ashlyn and Byrd Law Firm. Relationship-wise, Sinclair's college sweetheart decided to end the relationship once she finished her internship just a few months after his proposal.

As he sat in his office looking over a case, his assistant buzzed him.

"Mr. Tate, Peaches Davenport is on line three," she said.

"Thanks, Vanessa. Place her through," Sinclair said.

"Good afternoon, Sin. Did I catch you at a bad time?" Peaches asked as she unloaded her car from the Savannah trip.

"Never too busy for you, Peaches. What's up?"

"When are you back in Atlanta? I'm ready to file for divorce from Tristan?" she asked.

"I have to go out of the country for four days once I leave Seattle then back to Atlanta from there," he informed her.

"I really would like to be free of him and this marriage by the time I go on my Cabo trip with a few friends of mine. Is there anything I can do to get the ball rolling?" she asked.

"We could file a Notice of Publication; the notice would appear in the newspaper for two weeks, then a waiting period of forty-five days. Following that, the court will notify you to come down to get your final decree. As you know, I'll hold your hand through the entire process."

"Sounds great, Sin. Let's do it then." she insisted.

"I'll get right on it," Sinclair said.

"Thanks, Sin, I love you!"

"Love you as well, Peaches. Have a good day!" he said, ending the call.

✷ ✷ ✷

It was a beautiful Sunday morning, so I decided to cook breakfast, sit on the lanai, and stream church before I nestled on my sofa beneath my hand-knitted afghan to watch the third season of Netflix's *Grace and Frankie*. Three episodes in, I had two proposals to leave the house; one was from one of my graduates wanting to meet for an early lunch to discuss her career path after passing the board. The second call was from Lady T wanting to go to a matinee to see the movie *Split*. I declined both. I really wanted to binge this season of my favorite Netflix show. Midway through episode six, Lashawn called.

"Hey what's up?" I answered the phone.

"Uh oh, what are you doing? I feel like I'm about to be rushed off the phone," Lashawn said.

"I'm binge-watching a series on Netflix, but I'm pausing it to give you my undivided attention," I said.

"Just letting you know I've made my final payment to Blue Horizon Travel Agency for this trip you have us going on to Cabo," she said, sighing into the phone.

"Denise and Peaches have paid their balance as well. Haven't spoken with the other girls yet," I said.

"Alexis called me earlier. I will call her back and see what's up with her and let you get back to your show, sir," Lashawn said.

"Alright, ma'am, I love you. Have a good day. Kiss my babies and tell my nephew/son hello," I said, ending the call.

Eli walked in screaming as if he had exciting news. He had been out with friends after church. "Tyler! Where are you?" asked Eli.

"I'm in the den watching tv," I answered.

"Can you pause it a minute? I have some exciting news!"

"What's the urgency? Breathe!" I said.

"I found a house within my price range. If all goes well with the seller, I should be able to close in less than a month," he said.

"Nice, congratulations," I replied, feeling my mood suddenly tank.

"Why the solemn face if you're happy for me?" he asked.

"I'm happy for you. It's just you just moved in, and I have gotten used to you being here. I didn't think it would be so soon."

"I like being with you too, but I also want my own place that I can call home," he said.

"I get it. I really get it, and I am happy for you. Who is going to cook for me though?" I asked, laughing.

"I'll still cook for me, for you, for us," he said.

"Breakfast, lunch and dinner?" I asked jokingly.

"Look, sir, this will be good because I'm all over you, and I'm sure you could use the space. You seem to be doing a lot with your friends, and I don't want to impose on that," he said.

"You are not imposing, Eli. I go hang out with my friends when I want to, and you hang out with yours."

"Tyler, I'm going to let you get back to your show. I've got to make some phone calls. We can go out for dinner tonight if you'd like. I don't feel like cooking today."

"That's fine. I'm like four episodes from being finished. Maybe by then I'll be ready to eat and can decide what I have a taste for, cool?" I asked.

"Sounds good," he said.

"Again, congratulations, babe," I said, turning my show back on, only to be interrupted by a call from Isabella who was crying hysterically. "Hey, Isabella, how are you, my beautiful wife?" I asked.

"Not.... so good Tyler. Grandma passed this morning," she cried.

"Oh, babe, I am so sorry." My heart broke for Isabella. "When do we need to try to go home?" I asked.

"We? You mean you'll go with me?" she asked.

"Of course, I will. I wouldn't want you to travel alone during this time. I know you have your brother back in Portugal, but that's what friends are for. You were there for me when Will passed," I said.

"Let me pull myself together and call Tadeo back. I'll let you know what we decide about her arrangements, so you'll know when I plan to leave, and I'll take care of the airfare," she insisted.

"Just know I'm here for you in whatever way you need. We can say she lived a long life; much longer than what the doctors had given her," I said with a smile.

"That's so true. She did," Isabella said, and I knew that thought had given her some comfort.

"Praying for your strength. Let me know once arrangements are made. Love you," I said.

"Love you too, Tyler. Talk with you soon."

I walked into the bedroom to find Eli asleep with his mobile still in his hand.

"Hey babe, sorry to wake you. What's the combination to your safe; I need to get my passport out?" I asked.

"Why do you need your passport? Your Cabo trip isn't for another couple of months."

"My friend, Isabella's mom passed this morning. I'm flying to Portugal with her for support."

"Wait a minute. You're going where and to do what?" Eli asked. "My condolences to your friend, Tyler, but you are flying somewhere that you really know nothing about with people you really don't know?" he asked.

"It's not like that. I do know her, and can you just give me the combination or open it for me?" I asked starting to regret that I put my things in his safe.

"We aren't going to have a discussion about this? You just make up your mind, and that's it?" he asked. "What are we doing here, Tyler?"

"Pardon me, what do you mean what are we doing?" I asked.

"You make all these plans and trips with your friends. You're on the phone with Peaches nearly all day long every day, and you barely have time for me. The only intimacy I get from you is you holding me. We haven't had sex since I moved in!" he yelled.

"Why are you tripping?" I asked.

"I ain't trippin.' Tyler is in a relationship with Tyler. I guess I'm just here for the sake of you having a boyfriend, huh?" he asked. "The combination is sixty-nine, ten, eight. Get your passport, and I'm done, and to think I wanted to marry your selfish and crazy ass!" Eli screamed.

What Eli said didn't sit well with me, but I decided to give him some space for now. I walked into the closet to the safe, opened it, and got my passport. I pulled down the luggage to put it in the outer pocket then went back to watching tv. In the middle of the week, I flew to Portugal with Isabella. When I returned home, Eli had moved out with no warning. I tried calling him, but he wouldn't answer my call or return any of my texts.

To ease the hurt of losing Eli, eventually, I decided to call Sinclair.

"Hello Sinclair, this is Tyler. I know it has been a minute since we've spoken, but I'm open to having that tea if you're still open to that. Give me a call," I left a message, and my phone rang five minutes later.

"Greetings Tyler; I received your message and am both elated and shocked to hear from you," Sinclair said. "I'd love to see you, but since you put me off so long, I will choose the place." He laughed.

"Cool, just let me know when, and I'll be there," I said.

"Be dressed at 7 p.m. Text me your address, and I'll pick you up," he said.

"Well, you know the area where I live. Just meet me where you saw me walking my dog at 7 p.m. tonight. Baby steps, sir." I chuckled.

"You want to have it your way, don't you? See you at seven," Sinclair said.

"Totally forgot I have an engagement with some friends tonight, raincheck?" I asked.

"Have a good afternoon, Tyler. Call me when you're ready," he said, hanging up.

CHAPTER TEN

Come Back to Me

Alexis's marriage wasn't being dissolved fast enough, so she found a law firm that came highly recommended by a coworker. "Good morning and welcome to Ashlyn and Bird," said the receptionist, once she walked in.

"Hello, I'm Alexis Parker. I have an eleven o'clock appointment," she said.

"Mr. Sandlin, your eleven o'clock appointment is here to see you," announced the receptionist over the intercom.

Seconds later, Mr. Sandlin stepped out of his office and greeted Alexis in the waiting area. "Mrs. Parker, I'm Connor. Nice to meet you. Let's head back to my office," he said after a firm handshake.

"Mind if I use the ladies' room first?" she asked.

"Sure, it's right there on your left, and my office is two doors down on your right," he said.

Walking toward the restroom, Alexis noticed a gentleman enter Connor's office. She finished up her business in the bathroom and walked into her new lawyer's office. "My case isn't that bad that I'll need two handsome gentlemen to take it for me, is it?" she said, making light of her situation.

"Mrs. Parker, this is my colleague, Sinclair Tate. Due to my workload, he's agreed to take your case for me as he has more time to commit to handling it if that's fine with you?" Connor asked.

"Good morning, Mrs. Parker, I assure you that you will be in great hands with me. I'll make sure you get all you deserve," Sinclair said, extending his hand.

"I trust you." She smiled.

"Perfect! Let's walk across the hall to my office. Mr. Sandlin has given me your file, and we can finish where he left off," Sinclair instructed.

"Fine, thanks and nice meeting you Mr. Sandlin," Alexis said.

"Have a seat, Mrs. Parker," Sinclair said once we were inside his office, which was almost identical in style and design as Connor's. Both men liked dark leather and rich design.

"You can call me Alexis if you don't mind?"

"Alexis, call me Sinclair please."

"Deal," she confirmed.

"Now, let's get you divorced. Are you one hundred percent sure that's what you want to do?"

"I'm absolutely sure!" she yelled.

"I am looking over your folder, so no kids involved. Any properties? Are you seeking alimony or anything?" he asked.

"No, not at all, just my freedom!" she said.

"Well, this will be very easy. I'll have you sign some forms, and you pay a retainer. We file, and you should be a free woman in about thirty days. Fair enough?" Sinclair asked.

"Yes sir, let's do this," she said eagerly.

"Let me grab those forms for you. Would you like something to drink?" he asked.

"No thanks; I'm fine. Will I be able to make the payment with a credit card?" she asked.

"Yes, you can. Be right back." Sinclair got up and walked out of the office. "Sorry about the wait. Here are the forms I will need you to complete. Once you're done, I'll have my assistant come in to process your retainer," Sinclair said.

"No, I will go ahead and make payment in full, if that's fine with you?" she asked.

"That is perfectly alright. I'll give you a moment to finish and be right back," Sinclair said.

"Thanks, I will be done in about five minutes," Alexis said with a smile, happy that part of her life was finally coming to a close.

* * *

I called Alexis while she was still in the lawyer's office.

"Hey there. What are you up to?" I asked, wanting to see how things were going.

"I'm finishing up at the law firm. Give me about twenty minutes, and I'll call back," she said in a giddy tone.

"This is for the divorce, right?" I asked.

"Yes, and the way my lawyer is talking, I will be a free woman, and we can celebrate my divorce being final before our trip!" She laughed with excitement.

"Winner!" I said.

"Yes sir, I'll call you shortly. I need to get on your books anyway," she said.

"Chat with you soon, smooches," I said and hung up.

Eli and I hadn't spoken since he moved out, but we were invited to one of my close friend's wedding while we were a couple. I'd called Alexis to talk to her about it. She was unable to talk, but I was glad to hear her news. My phone rang, and it was the call I'd been dreading.

"Hello."

"Hey Tyler, how's it going? I see you haven't confirmed your hotel reservation for you and Eli. Will you be staying at the host hotel or have you decided on a different one?" Stacia asked.

I didn't want to tell her we were no longer a couple, so I went with, "I'm still waiting on him to let me know if he got approved for the days off, but I'll go online and book it today," I said.

"What day will you be in town, so I can arrange for LA of Dallas to do my hair and makeup?" she asked.

"I'm coming in on Friday morning. We are doing your hair and makeup for your photo shoot Saturday afternoon, correct?" I asked.

"Yes, and perfect! Now I can relax and breathe," she sighed.

"You're too funny. You know I've got you covered. What are you doing?" I asked.

"Sitting on the patio drinking some Harney and Son's black tea with freshly baked, organic blueberry muffins," she answered.

"Sounds delish! I'll see you soon, and enjoy your afternoon. Smooches," I said.

I attempted to reach Eli via text and voicemail to see if he was still attending Stacia's wedding, but I got no response from him. I decided not to reach out to him about it anymore. I would just attend, honor my obligations, and enjoy the day as best I could.

On the day of the wedding, I was shocked to receive a call from Eli.

"Hey you," Eli said.

"Hello there, how are you?" I asked.

"I'm downstairs awaiting you in the Town Car to take us to the wedding. How long before you come down?" he asked.

Taken aback, I stopped and glared at the phone. Was he serious?

"Uh, I didn't think you were coming since I hadn't heard from you," I told him.

"I didn't want you to be without a date for the awaited moment of your dearest friend to wed the man of her dreams," he said.

"I'll be down in three minutes," I said before grabbing my bag and taking the elevator feeling relieved and a bit excited.

The ceremony was an intimate one of about a hundred guests with beautiful florals arranged by the bride's mom; the colors were cream, ivory, and gold. All the women wore ivory or cream dresses, and the men wore black tuxedos. Eli was dapper in his Hickey Freeman tuxedo, Hugo Boss patent shoes, a crisp ivory shirt, and a black pocket square and lapel pin.

After the ceremony, the guests were asked to go to the banquet room for the reception and take their assigned seats with their name cards on the table. I met the bride in the changing room to take her updo to a side chignon to go with the wardrobe change she had to greet her guests for the reception.

"Everything is so beautiful, and you made a lovely bride. Tastefully done," I said.

"Thanks, and you've made my day special by doing my hair and having Lacey do my makeup. LA of Dallas, y'all are a bad duo! Give me a high five," Stacia said.

"My pleasure, so glad I was able to be a part of this day," I admitted.

"Oh my God! This chignon is just as beautiful as the updo. When I get back from my honeymoon, we must start planning you and Eli's wedding. He looks so handsome today," she said.

"Glad you love it! I'll head out and wait for you to come out. Kisses," I said, making no mention that Eli and I were separated.

The reception was also tastefully done. Being that it was early Sunday afternoon, there were waffles, biscuits, omelets, fruit and a variety of breakfast meats with mimosas, sangrias, and bellinis. I enjoyed myself immensely until it was time to leave. Eli and I took the Town Car back to the hotel and sat at the bar. Not long after he drank his third dirty martini, he said, "Let's go up to my room so we can finish talking without the loud sound of the piano playing in the background."

"Sure, that sounds good. But we can go to my room," I said, standing to walk upstairs.

Once we reached my door, he spared no time looking into my eyes and pouring out his heart.

"Tyler, I've really missed you, and I need the hurt you've caused me to go away. I love you like family and for you to have no regard for me caring about you, wanting the best for you, and just some consideration and communication was hurtful."

"I just couldn't understand why you blew up like you did and to call me selfish and crazy, what the fuck, Eli!" I yelled.

"I have forgiven you, and I want to work on a friendship because you are a good person, a bad boyfriend but a good person." He leaned in to kiss me, and I didn't resist it.

Deep down inside, I knew Eli was right. I wasn't ready to give him all that he required in a relationship. "I'd like the friendship, as well," I said, pulling away from the kiss.

Eli jumped back from me, and a wave of guilt covered his handsome facial features.

"I didn't mean to do that, forgive me," he apologized as he left heading to his room.

My heart raced, and my dick throbbed in my extra slim-fit tuxedo pants that I was ready to pry off because I longed to lay next to him and feel his body.

I undressed to start my shower, and there was a knock at the adjacent door to mine. I was startled at first but decided to satisfy my curiosity to ask, "Who is it?"

Eli replied, "It's me, Tyler. Open the door."

To my surprise, he was standing in the door between our rooms with only his briefs. I looked into those sleepy eyes then down to his soft lips and hairy chest. My eyes moved down to see a hint of jumping action in his Psycho Bunny briefs. I pulled Eli into the room and led him to my bed, massaging his smooth head as he kissed me uncontrollably.

"Turn around." He pushed my face into the bed.

"What are you doing?" I asked.

"Be quiet. Hmmm, I see you went and got your manzilian waxing," he said as I felt his tongue swipe across my flesh.

Eli and I made love until sunrise, both appreciating each other in ways like never before.

At 7:25 a.m., the sun beamed beyond the curtains, and I awakened to find my bed was empty. I called Eli's name thinking he was in the bathroom. I crawled out of bed only to notice he was not in my room any longer, and his side of the adjacent door was now locked.

I took a shower, got dressed, and headed to the front desk to check out, thinking Eli was either at the gym or waiting on me downstairs.

The front desk clerk asked, "How was your stay? Mr. Thomas left a note for you." She handed me the note and finished checking me out. "I called your town car. It will be here in five minutes," she added.

"Thank you." I walked over to stand by the couch in the lobby to read the letter Eli wrote to me:

Tyler, I feel bad for leaving so early, but I had to. I'm glad that we were able to spend this time together and wish we could be more than friends. Keep in touch…Love, Eli.

I grabbed my bag to head to the car. I called Bobbie and told her what happened. She conferenced Alexis on our call.

"Hey babe, are you okay?" Alexis asked.

"No, he isn't okay, but he could be if he would stop being stubborn and just tell Eli the truth!" Bobbie screamed.

"Before you tear into me, may I at least talk?" I asked.

"Can someone tell me what's going on?" Alexis asked.

"Hold on." I held the phone away from my ear and told the driver, "I'm heading to DFW Airport, Delta Airlines."

"He's dodging me, Alexis," Bobbie said.

"No, I'm not. I just want to make sure I make it to catch my flight back home," I said.

"I'm lost," Alexis said.

"Tyler let Eli end their relationship because he didn't tell him the reason he flew to Portugal with Isabella wasn't only to show her support but because they're still married and thought the family would wonder why her husband didn't come," Bobbie blurted.

"Tyler, I thought you and her had filed for divorce?" Alexis asked.

"No, over the years I totally forgot all about it. It crossed my mind a few times after Will died and Da Wife was the one recognized as his spouse *and* next of kin by his family and the military; I became numb to filing the divorce," I said.

"Now, with Isabella's grandmother recently passing, he can rightfully divorce her as they planned," Bobbie said.

"I'm going to look into that this week; I promise," I said.

"Well, I have a wonderful attorney that helped me with mine, and it was so easy. Since you guys don't have any kids, property or finances together, it will be over quickly," Alexis said.

"Send me the number, and I'll make the appointment and take his ass myself!" Bobbie screamed.

"I wanted to talk with you two about the course of the day and night of the wedding and after with Eli, but Bobbie wants to hound me about this divorce. I've made it to the airport and will discuss it later," I said, exhausted.

"Oh, so now you want to be sensitive. You Geminis don't have emotions or a heart. You're not hurt," Bobbie laughed.

"Alexis, make the appointment and text me the address and time I'm to show up," I said.

"And text me too, Alexis. I'm going. Tyler have a safe flight and call me when you land. Love you, babe," Bobbie said.

"Love you girls more," I said, ending the call.

CHAPTER ELEVEN

HE WON'T GO

Peaches realized she allowed too much time to pass without seeing her parents, so she decided to catch a flight to surprise them for their anniversary party. When she got the rental car and pulled out of the airport parking garage, she called her old neighbor Mandy.

"Hello, Mandy, is now a good time to chat?" Peaches asked.

"Yes, Peaches, how are you?" Mandy asked.

"I'm well thanks for asking. I know I abruptly left that night but didn't want to get you involved. I need a favor if you will?" Peaches asked.

"Sure, girl anything. What do you need?" Mandy asked.

"Tristan usually leaves the house around five fifteen in the morning and returns after eight p.m. I'm going to send you the garage door code, and you will find two boxes in the right corner of the garage behind a screen divider. Could you grab them and meet me with them today? I'd like to get them and ship them while I'm there," Peaches asked.

"I'm pulling in the subdivision in three minutes. Send me the code and the address to meet you," Mandy said.

"Thanks, girl. You're the greatest!" Peaches said.

"I'm just glad to be able to help, and I'm glad you finally left him," Mandy said. An hour later, Mandy met Peaches at the post office where they hugged for what seemed like an hour. "What happened? Why did you leave so abruptly that night?" Mandy asked.

"When you said, 'I heard screaming and thought I should call the police,' Tristan had me up against the wall by the neck, I was losing my breath, and he told me he would kill me. He only had one time to say that to me," Peaches said.

"Oh, wow girl. I'm sorry to hear that. Are you okay now though?" Mandy asked.

"Girl, I am having the time of my life. I'm divorced, have made some wonderful friends, and having my first girls' trip in addition to a male friend that's like a brother named Tyler. We are going to Cabo. That's why I needed these boxes; I have some cute pieces in there that Tristan would have a fit had I wore them."

"Sounds like fun! Max and I are expecting our second child; it's a girl this time. He's so happy, but I wanted to be the only princess in the house," Mandy said, and laughter erupted from her small frame.

"I was going to ask you to go out with me to my dad's lounge tonight. They're having their anniversary party, but you can't drink," Peaches said.

"No, I can't drink, but I can dance. I love your parents, and it will be great to see them. Do they know you're in town?" Mandy asked.

"No, they have no idea. Did you want to meet there or ride together?" Peaches asked.

"I'll pick you up. Send me the information about where you are staying. I've got to head home so the sitter can leave; she has probably put Ryan down for his nap by now," Mandy said.

"Okay, I'll send you the information. Let's plan to leave around seven-ish," Peaches said.

* * *

When Mandy walked in with Peaches behind her later that night, Peaches' father had a face of uncontrollable tears as his beautiful daughter approached him with a white linen, nearly sheer, skirt and a white tank that met just enough to reveal a portion of the tattoo of Peaches along her panty line. He grabbed her and held her as if it was to save his life.

"Oh, my goodness. How's Daddy's girl?" Joseph asked, pulling her into his office.

"Dad, I'm fine. Life is great for me. I'm divorced. I have a gig in Atlanta and hope to get a connect where I can put out an album one day soon," Peaches relayed.

"Baby, where are you staying? How long are you here?" he asked.

"At the moment, Sinclair has taken me in, and I leave out tomorrow morning. I came in today just for your anniversary party," she said.

"That's so sweet of you. Where are you staying while you're here? I'll have Maxine fix the guestroom for you," he said.

"No need. I'm staying at a hotel near the airport so that I can drop the car off and be on my way back."

"Let me just sit and look in my daughter's eyes to ensure she is really alright." Joseph sat back in his chair, and his dark oval eyes peered into his daughter's looking for evidence of her wellbeing.

"Dad, I'm really good, I promise. Now, let's get out here and celebrate you and Maxine!"

One of the bartenders knocked on the door to share with her father that he needed to grab a couple of bottles of Svedka to restock the shelf. He noticed Peaches in the chair.

"Peaches, hey beautiful! We miss you. I know you're going to sing for us at least one song tonight, right?" the bartender asked.

"Yes, baby; sing at least one song for us tonight," Joseph chimed in.

"For you, dad, I can't resist."

"Well, that's settled. Tell the musician to get ready to set up our Peaches Graces the Stage setup," Joseph told the bartender.

"I just left poor Mandy when you pulled me away from her. Let me get out to her," Peaches said and left out of her father's office with her father following her.

"Mandy, pardon my manners, and thanks for coming to bring my baby. Have any drink you want on the house," Joseph said.

"Thanks, Mr. Davenport, but I will have to decline. I'm expecting." Mandy blushed.

"Congratulations to you and Max. Come on; have a seat. Peaches is about to perform a song," Joseph said before walking up to the stage area. "Ladies and gentleman, please welcome to the stage my beautiful songstress, Peaches."

The crowd erupted in cheers as Joseph handed his daughter the mic.

Mandy, Joseph, Maxine, and the rest of her family sat at the tables close to the stage as Peaches opened her mouth to sing Heather Headley's "In My Mind," not knowing she was being recorded on Facebook Live by a patron of the lounge.

Peaches' husband watched from his device at home and threw on some black joggers, a shirt, and some sneakers, heading to Bus Boys & Poets before she finished her third song.

"Peaches! Peaches, I need to talk to you!" Tristan yelled from the crowd.

"Tristan, I'm not having that in my bar tonight. I'm going to have to ask you to leave, son," Joseph said.

"Dad, I just need five minutes with my wife," Tristan pleaded.

"Maxine, take Peaches and Mandy to the office," Joseph said.

"I just need to apologize to my wife. Just five minutes," Tristan begged.

"She's your ex-wife, and when you threatened my daughter's life, you lost all rights to talk to or be near her. Please, let's do this cordially. Leave my bar now. Security, will you come escort this gentleman out of here." Joseph waved as security carried a yelling and kicking Tristan away. He walked into the office to find Peaches crying. "It's alright, baby girl. He's gone."

"How did he know I was here? I'm sorry to have ruined your night, Dad and Maxine," Peaches sobbed.

"It's not your fault. You can't take ownership for his foolishness," Mandy said.

"Dad, if you and Maxine are good, I'm going to get Mandy to take me on to my room, so I can try to rest before my flight in the morning. Again, I'm sorry."

"Peaches, we understand. I'm just grateful you came, and you're doing alright," Maxine said.

"Let me grab something out of my drawer. I will walk you ladies to the car," Joseph said.

"Maxine, I love you. Happy Anniversary, and take care of this young man for me," Peaches said.

"You take care of yourself, and let us know when you're back in Atlanta safely," Maxine said.

"Baby, I'll be right back. I'm walking them to the car," Joseph said to Maxine.

"Okay, good seeing you Mandy," Maxine said.

"Dre, come spot me as I walk my girls to the car to see them off," Joseph said to his security guard.

"Yes sir, Mr. Davenport. I noticed Tristan take off about ten minutes ago," Dre said.

"Dad, I love you. Enjoy the rest of your anniversary party. The crowd is jumping, so I don't think anyone really noticed," Peaches said.

"I'm not worried about the crowd. I'm worried about you and Mandy's safety. Mandy, I'm going to call Max. I want him waiting on you when you pull in; I'm not sure with the commotion if Tristan saw you here," Joseph said.

"Thanks, Mr. Davenport, but I'll be fine. I echo Peaches. Enjoy the remainder of your night," Mandy said.

"I'm calling him anyway, young lady. And, for you Peaches, I want you to call me as soon as you get inside of your hotel."

"I will, Dad. He's gone home. I'll be fine."

Peaches arrived at her hotel and called her father to let her know she was safe. That would be the last time she ever saw Tristan.

CHAPTER TWELVE

IMAGINE

After contemplating whether to go or not to go, I kept the appointment Alexis made for me to go see her attorney to file for divorce. I really didn't want to have this conversation with Isabella yet. She was still mourning the loss of her grandmother.

"Good afternoon. My name is Tyler, and I have a 2 p.m. appointment with Mr. Tate," I told the lawyer's smiling receptionist.

"I will let him know you are here. Do you care for something to drink?" she asked as footsteps could be heard coming up the hallway made of gray polished quartzite tile.

Our eyes met when the footsteps stopped.

"Tyler?" Sinclair asked.

"Sinclair, I'm your two o'clock appointment?" I answered quizzically.

"Yes, you are. Follow me this way," he said.

"I had no idea you were an attorney," I said as I entered his office that was decorated with his credentials on the walls.

"Have a seat. Funny having you here. What is this about? You cancel our date, and now you're here filing for divorce. I'm confused," he said in a sincere tone.

"It is a bit complicated, but I will start with my good friend Alexis Parker. She spoke highly of you and made the appointment for me because another one of my friends insists on me getting a divorce, so I can be free of my marriage," I said.

"Don't be offended by this question. I just want to know for my own personal accord. Are you married to a man or woman?" he asked.

"A woman. Her grandmother's last wish was to see her marry, so we did it about ten years ago for her one-hundredth birthday. I married my friend because she wanted to give her grandmother a last request of seeing her married before she died, but her grandmother went on to live eight more years," I explained.

"That's really interesting, Tyler. I really want to help you with your case, but I have a personal interest in you so I'd rather have my business partner handle your case. He was actually supposed to handle your friend's case, but his load was too busy, so he handed her over to me. Are you okay with that?" he asked.

"Do I have a choice?" I asked.

"I'd like to keep your business here at the firm, but I have a personal interest in having a proper date with you, so I'd rather let Connor handle it." His heated gaze spoke volumes.

"That's fine, Sinclair," I said. I wanted him to be my lawyer. I also wanted to explore the possibility of where a date could take us.

Sinclair picked up his phone. "Connor, mind coming into my office a minute please?"

"Knock, knock. What's up, guy?" a man, who I assumed was Connor, asked.

"Connor, I called you in here because a good friend of our client, Alexis Parker, is here, and he will need your representation. I would handle his case, but there's a conflict of interest. Tyler, I'd like to introduce you to Connor," Sinclair said, nodding at Connor.

"Pleasure to meet you, Tyler. Come on up to my office so we can discuss how I can assist you," Connor said.

"Thanks, Sinclair. Have a good day," I said.

"Tyler, I need that date this week," Sinclair said for my ears only.

I smiled and left out of his office following Connor.

"Have a seat and tell me what's going on so I can help you, sir," said Connor.

"I've been married since 2009. My wife and I are on good terms. There's no property, kids or finances to be considered. I'd like to file for divorce and end this marriage as soon as possible," I divulged.

"You've answered a few of my main questions, but I'd like to know if you two live in the same house, or is she in another city or state?" Connor asked.

"No, we've never lived together, and she lives here."

"Let me get you to go over this paperwork. If your wife cooperates, we can file the petition-and you can be divorced within thirty days," Connor assured me.

"She will cooperate, and that's great news," I said.

After I completed my paperwork and made the payment, I sent Isabella a text to call me. I wanted her to hear it from me before being served papers. My phone rang as soon as I walked out of the lawyer's office.

"Hello?"

"Tyler, this is Sinclair. I have a request of you, and I'm not taking no for an answer."

"I'm listening."

"I would be honored if you'd accompany me for a work function this weekend. What say you?"

"I'm going to say yes and keep my word this time," I said.

"Perfect!" Sinclair gasped.

"What are the details?" I asked.

"It is a black-tie event. I will arrange for you to be picked up by midday on Friday with a light snack in the car on the way to the airport as I will have lunch prepared for you once you arrive in Seattle," Sinclair said.

"Hold up, car, flight, Seattle?" I asked.

"Yes, sir. You really don't have to bring anything unless there's something personal you'd like," he said nonchalantly.

"Well, you said it's a black tie, so I'll at least need my tux and shoes," I said.

"Not really. You're a forty regular jacket, about a fifteen and a half shirt with thirty-four length sleeve, thirty-three large pants, and I'm guessing a size eleven and a half shoe, right?" he asked.

"Exactly, have you been in my closet?" I laughed.

"I've studied you enough to know your frame, so I will have everything you need on Friday."

"Is that so?" I asked.

"Yes, sir. Meet my driver where I met you walking and where I was supposed to pick you up two weeks ago around 10:45 a.m. on Friday. I'll email you the flight itinerary," he said.

"Is this a joke, Sinclair?" I asked.

"Not at all, man. I've been trying to get your hard to get self for nearly a year. I'm not letting an opportunity slip through my fingers again," he said.

"If you say so," I digressed.

"See you in Seattle on Friday." He ended the call, and three days later, his driver picked me up and dropped me off at the airport to head to Seattle.

I called Denise to tell her where I was going and let her know I would call her once I'd arrived safely. A driver was awaiting me at the Seattle airport to take me to Sinclair's home. He pulled up to Sinclair's home and parked. Then, he got out of the car, opened the door for me, and grabbed my luggage out of the car. He escorted me to the front door and rang the bell for me.

"Mr. Tate, I will see you gentlemen this evening around six p.m. Enjoy your afternoon," the driver said when Sinclair opened the door.

"What an impressive start to a first date. Thanks for all of the details of transporting this precious cargo here." I laughed.

"Did both of my drivers take great care of you? And how was your flight?" he asked.

"Yes, they did, and the flight was long but smooth. Thanks for everything," I said.

"Let me take your bag, and may I have a hug?" he asked.

"Sure." I wrapped my arms around him, and we embraced like old friends and lovers.

A moan escaped Sinclair as he said, "You give good hugs. I can get used to those. Help yourself to a seat on the back porch, and I'll put your bag away and join you in a moment."

Sinclair had a beautiful lunch prepared for the two of us. We sat on the porch facing the lake, and I was in awe when I walked out to see the crisp linen-covered table with a vase of bromeliads along with two covered dishes, a bottle of wine being chilled on ice, and the sounds of Tamia's "Careless Whisper" playing through the Bose speakers.

"How is everything?" Sinclair asked. He removed the lid to the dishes, and there was pan-seared quail with roasted, rosemary potatoes and grilled asparagus. We enjoyed the breeze from the lake as we witnessed a few people kayaking and the sounds of the birds chirping around them.

"How do you leave this place? It's so peaceful here," I said, basking in the beauty of the scenery.

"Well, most of my friends are in Atlanta, and my parents are in Florida which is closer to Atlanta. I just helped a good friend out of an unhealthy situation, so she's staying in my condo in Atlanta until she gets on her feet," he replied thoughtfully.

"You are a great friend. Mmmm," I savored a bite of rosemary potatoes. "Did you prepare this delicious meal yourself, or did you have Rosita do it?" I teased.

"I can cook, sir. I prepared it myself," he said.

"And no shade about Rosita," I said.

"None taken. Do you want seconds?" he asked.

"No, I'm full. Everything was delicious. Let me clear the table."

"Tyler, you sit right there and relax. I'd like you to get used to this, so this can one day be yours," he said and walked into the kitchen, leaving me wondering what he meant by that. This was our first date, yet I felt comfortable with him as if we had history. "Tyler, I need to run into the office to finish something before the gala tonight. Come let me show you the guest room if you don't feel comfortable sleeping with me," he said from the doorway.

"I'll sleep in the guest room," I said, thinking *baby steps sir.*

Sinclair showed me a room that was as big as a great room. It was equipped with a king-size bet, a chaise lounger, and enough space to host a yoga class.

Wow, this is the life, I wanted to say, but all I said was, "This is beautiful."

"Alright, sir, make yourself comfortable, and I'll be back shortly. Get some rest, and thanks again for coming to be my date tonight," said Sinclair.

"You're welcome. I'm excited, and thanks for the invite. Be safe, see you shortly, Sinclair."

He looked as if he wanted to say more... to do more, but he just turned on his heels and walked out of the room, leaving me alone. Just before laying down, I remembered I had a missed call from Eli, but I decided I would speak with him later.

Around 5 p.m., Sinclair knocked on the door telling me it was about time we started getting ready. I pulled myself out of bed and went into the shower. When I stepped out of the shower, laying on the bed next to my tuxedo and shirt were a pair of cuff links and a bracelet in a David Yurman box. The card read: *Tyler, to a wonderful man that I hope to have the pleasure of getting to know more and more each day.... Sinclair.*

As I walked down the hall, I saw Sinclair looking through the ceiling to floor glass window of his living room while fixing the collar to his ivory tuxedo jacket. He heard the clapping of my feet on the Brazilian cherry hardwood floors and turned around.

"Tyler, you look extremely handsome. I'm going to be the luckiest guy in the room tonight," he said.

"Thanks, Sinclair. Everything fits perfectly. I will wear the bracelet and cufflinks tonight, but I can't accept them."

"And why not? They're yours. If you don't feel you can accept them this weekend, we will put them in the master closet, and as you frequent here you're welcome to wear them when you're comfortable," he said.

"Fair enough and thank you. No, I will be the luckiest guy in the room tonight," I admitted.

As we looked in one another's eyes and checked our bowties, the doorbell rang. The driver was on the other side waiting to take us to the fundraiser banquet. At the car, the driver was heading to open the door for me when Sinclair said, "I have it."

I stepped in and slid over for him to sit beside me. He reached over and placed his hand on mine as we rode. "Thanks again for coming. I hope you enjoy tonight. If at any time you're uncomfortable or ready to go, pull your bow tie and we will leave, or I will have my driver bring you back to the house," Sinclair said.

A couple of hours into the ceremony, Sinclair was awarded for winning the most cases in the firm which made me proud of him. After dinner was served and a bit of mingling, Sinclair introduced me to a few of his colleagues and decided to dip out of the party and take me to a night club in downtown Seattle called R Place. We danced, shot pool, and karaoked over into the wee hours of the morning. The driver was awaiting us to step out of the club and took us back to Sinclair's house. When we made it to the house and I was walking towards the guest room, Sinclair whispered, "You don't have to sleep alone if you don't want to. I'll respect you enough not to be inappropriate. I do sleep nude, however, if that's not a problem for you."

"It's not a problem, but I do prefer we take things slow," I said.

"If that's what you want," Sinclair replied.

I followed his lead to his room where he held me until I drifted off to sleep. His bed was so comfortable that it felt like we were sleeping on cotton.

The next morning, I woke to the sun beaming through the windows. I wanted to pull the eighteen hundred thread count Egyptian sheets back over my head, but before I pulled the covers over my head, I spotted six hummingbirds at the feeder outside of Sinclair's window.

My phone was vibrating uncontrollably with text messages from Peaches for her daily check-in, and she wanted to schedule an appointment for her hair. I sent her a text telling her I was still on a high from last night and would call her later in the afternoon.

Sinclair waltzed into the room moments later wearing a pair of gym shorts and carrying a breakfast tray in hand. The tray had shrimp and grits, poached eggs, and a cup of Sanderson's English breakfast tea. "Good morning, handsome. How did you sleep?" he asked, giving me a kiss on the lips.

"I slept peacefully, thanks, and you?" I asked.

"It was hard sleeping with your warm, sexy body next to mine and resisting being inappropriate with you. I had to get up and put on some boxers," he said, laughing.

"My bad; I should have slept in the guest room," I said.

"Guest rooms are for guests. This will be your home, Tyler," he said.

"You're flattering; do you know that, Sinclair?"

"Yes, but it's true."

"How do you know we're going to make it past this date, much less stay together long enough for me to move in here?" I asked, spooning up some grits. "You're not eating?" I asked.

"I made me a shake after my morning run, but I just have this feeling that you're the one for me," he said, peering into my eyes.

I nodded. I couldn't deny that I felt safe with Sinclair. I wished I hadn't put him off for so long. "What time did you get up for your run?" I asked, changing the subject.

"Six every morning. If it's alright with you, I'm going to put on some music while I read over this case," he said.

"Sure."

Sinclair left the bedroom and, moments later, the sounds of Marion Hill played through the speakers. I crawled out of bed to take the tray to the kitchen and found him on what sounded like an urgent phone call.

"Yes Pops. I'll handle it and will call you this afternoon. Love you too," he said ending the call before I could pick up on what was bothering him.

I eased over to the sink to wash the dishes. "That was good. Thanks, Sinclair."

"Just leave it on the counter, babe. I just got some bad news. I had so much planned for us later this evening and tomorrow, but I need to get back to Florida to take care of an important family matter. Then, I have to go to the Barbados to finalize a property matter." He paused to gauge my response. "I would love it if you could come along with me for both."

"I'm sorry to hear that, Sinclair. Sounds like something big has happened," I probed.

"We can talk about it on the plane. Will you check your availability to see if you can go along with me? If not, I totally understand and can just fly you back to Atlanta when I leave out, and we can see one another when I get back," he said in a solemn tone.

"I would like to go with you, but I've had several clients call for appointments. I've ignored their calls because I'm enjoying my time with you," I said.

"Babe, I understand that you have to get back to work. Let me get online and look for us some flights right quick," he said.

"Is there anything I can do to take the stress off of you?" I asked.

"No, just go ahead and take your shower," he suggested.

I walked into the bathroom and Sinclair came in behind me. He turned on both shower heads in the six-foot-wide, glazed white porcelain shower with heated lamps; he pointed for me to get in. "Enjoy," he said as he turned on the towel warmer and tossed two plush white towels on them.

When I stepped out of the shower, the towels were warm.

"Leave it running, I'm about to jump in, and don't be looking down at my bulge. Sorry, you got me excited just by looking at you," he said. "I'll take care of this while you're getting dressed." Sinclair laughed it off, but in all honesty, the sexual attraction was mutual.

Moments later, we were both dressed and ready to leave. He armed the alarm. We walked to the car heading to the Seattle-Tacoma International Airport to board our flights to Atlanta and Orlando.

CHAPTER THIRTEEN

START ALL OVER

Eli tried to reach me to share some life-changing news, but I had been unavailable. He needed to speak with someone, so he called Bobbie as they had grown a great bond with one another.

"Hey Bobbie, how are you?" Eli asked.

"Hey, babe. All is well. How are you?" she asked.

"I need to talk with you about something. Are you available for an early dinner?" he asked.

"Let me get Morgan to pick Maia up from school, and I'll leave here in about thirty minutes if that's good for you?" she asked.

"Cool, how's Houston's in Buckhead, and dinner is on me?" he said.

"Hell, I can leave now if that's the case." She burst out in laughter.

"See you soon, and thanks so much. I tried calling your shady friend, Tyler, but he hasn't called me back yet," he sighed.

"We both know Tyler stays busy," Bobbie said before they said their goodbyes.

Eli arrived at the restaurant a few minutes before Bobbie. He took the liberty to order the salmon chips and a dirty martini as he awaited her arrival. She walked with her Pam Grier afro, strapless denim romper, and hot pink heels.

"Hey, beautiful! You look stunning today. Thanks again for meeting me," Eli said.

"Thanks and you look dapper, as always, with that Colgate smile," she complimented him.

"Excuse me, would you please bring the lady a glass of Riesling?" Eli asked the waitress.

"How did you know or remember that?" Bobbie asked.

"I recall Tyler getting a bottle when we came to celebrate you and Morgan."

"Great memory. You're so thoughtful," she added.

"I just want to have this sidebar before having the conversation I want to speak with you about. I really miss your smiling face and bubbly energy," he said.

"I miss you too, and you know that I've adopted you even though it didn't work out between you and Tyler. Although, I still feel like y'all haven't broken up." She laughed.

"Well, you know that twin side of his gets in his own way." Eli laughed nervously.

"I know, but we aren't going to talk about him. What's going on with you, sir?" Bobbie asked.

"I was dating this guy and ended up moving him in; you know, me being the nice person that I am. He had gotten locked up, lost his place, and became homeless. One day when I got home from work, he had taken my washer and dryer plus some of my winter coats, clothes, and shoes," Eli said.

Bobbie frowned. "That is messed up. He will reap what he has sewn. His due justice will come back around," she said.

"Then, today after all of the hard work and dedication I put into my job, going in extra early some mornings, working through lunch breaks, overtime, and occasional Saturdays to complete projects and meet the goals for the team, the company had the audacity to sever ties with me and give me hush money to keep me from taking them to court. I really don't know what to do," he said.

"Eli, you should really pursue the advice Tyler gave you and follow your niche of styling people and making those beautiful bracelets. Be your own boss and work for Eli," Bobbie said.

The server came back to take their order. "What can I get for you two?"

"You can go first, Bobbie," Eli said.

I'm really not hungry after eating this dip. I can have one more glass of Riesling though," she said.

"I will have another dirty martini, as well," Eli ordered. "Bobbie, I can't thank you enough for meeting with me."

"No problem, babe. Let's toast to new beginnings!"

CHAPTER FOURTEEN

GIVE ME WHAT I WANT

Denise and her husband, Lloyd, celebrated their twenty-second anniversary. Since she would be away on a trip with Tyler and the girls, she decided to plan a trip for the two of them to the Biltmore Estates in Asheville, NC.

"Baby, this is a really nice property. Good choice," Lloyd said.

"It came highly recommended by Lashawn. She came here for her anniversary one year," Denise said.

"How is she doing since the divorce?" Lloyd asked.

"She appears to be doing great. We had a great celebration for her, and she's looking forward to our Cabo trip in two weeks."

"Good for her. I know that damn Tyler is going to have you all doing all kinds of extra shit. He's not taking that guy Eli with you all, is he?" Lloyd asked.

"No, it's just us. He and Eli are no longer an item. As for being extra, we are to wear #beingmarriedtoher t-shirts one day." She laughed.

"That boy runs them all off, huh?" Lloyd said, laughing.

"You leave my friend alone. He's still finding himself," Denise said.

"Whatever. What do you want to do today?" Lloyd asked.

"I arranged for a wine tasting, horseback riding, and then dinner. Tomorrow we will have a light breakfast and tour the estate and city before returning back to Alabama," she replied.

"Somewhere in your plans, you'll be satisfying my needs for our anniversary, right?" he asked.

"Why of course, sir. I've got to reward my man for allowing me the opportunity to be away from him during our anniversary!" She batted her eyes and ran her tongue across her lips.

Hours after their wine tasting, horseback riding, and dinner, Lloyd grabbed his wife and said, "Daddy is ready to take Mommy back to the room."

"Mommy is ready for Daddy!" she moaned.

When they made it to the room, Denise decided she wanted to do something risqué. While he was in the restroom, she lifted her dress over her head and threw on a robe.

"Come here Daddy!" she whispered, leading her husband to the balcony of their room.

"What are you doing, Denise? On the balcony?" he asked with a smile.

"Yes, sir!" She dropped her robe and started gyrating her hips while biting her bottom lip. She turned her back to him, and he pushed her over the balcony rail and used his right foot to spread her legs apart. He grabbed the back of her hair and pulled her in. Then, he put his left hand around her neck.

"Who does this pussy belong to?" he asked while he slowly slid his hard penis into her vaginal walls from behind. Lloyd lifted her up, turning her around to press her against the wall. He continued making love to her until they climaxed.

"I love you! Happy fucking anniversary. Give me my dick, Daddy!" she yelled, forgetting they were outside.

CHAPTER FIFTEEN

FREAK ME BABY

Bobbie buttered up her husband and daughter for keeping Maia while she went on her getaway to Cabo with her crew. "Here Kie, I made an appointment for you to get your hair done. Head on over to Tyler's salon; he's expecting you," she said.

"Really Mom. Is he doing the braidless sew in?" Kie asked.

"Yes, now be on your way. You know how particular he is about promptness," Bobbie said.

"Thanks, Mom. I love you! I'll take great care of Maia while you are away," Kie screamed.

Now that she'd gotten her daughter out of the house, and Maia was still in school, she went downstairs to the family room with nothing on but an oversized shirt. She stood in front of the television while Morgan was watching it.

"Bobbie, what are you doing? I'm watching the game..." he said, taking his wife's seductive pose.

She pressed the record button then turned the tv off. At the same time, she removed the shirt above her head. She walked over to Morgan and got on both knees. She reached in the center of his lounge pants to feel her mission was accomplished; his throbbing dick was awakened.

"There are better things you could be doing right now instead of watching a boring game," she whispered.

"And what could be better than watching a game?" he asked, leaning back on the sofa.

She sucked his dick into her hot mouth.

"Ahhhhh, Bobbie, shit that feels so good," he moaned. The more he moaned, the faster and deeper she took him in her mouth. He whispered, "Feed me, baby."

She stood on her right leg as she put her left leg up on the head of the sofa. She sat on his face so he could eat her freshly sugared vagina compliments of Sugar Lips in Buckhead.

He couldn't stop eating her. He moaned, "Damn your pussy tastes and feels so good against my mouth."

Bobbie turned around to face the mirror on the adjacent wall and slid down her husband's throbbing manhood. Sliding up and down on his erection, she played with her pussy.

"Morgan, you've got me so freakin' wet. I feel like a fountain," she said as she rode him until they both exploded. They went upstairs to shower together, making love again when something arose in her husband.

Completely spent by the passion he'd just shared with his wife, Morgan whispered in her ear, "Whatever it is that you did to your pussy, I like that. Let's keep that up."

CHAPTER SIXTEEN

ON BENDED KNEE

~Los Cabos Day One~

The day had finally come for me and my angels to take flight for our trip to Los Cabos. I arrange a shuttle for me, Denise, Lashawn, and Alexis to the airport as Peaches and Bobbie rode together. We were all very excited wearing our #beingmarriedtoher t-shirts and recording play by play of us cutting up at the gate until we boarded the plane and was instructed to turn our phones off or put them in airplane mode. When we arrived at SJD airport, our personal driver awaited us with a sign that read 'Tyler's Angels.'

"Lord, you're too much, sir," Lashawn said, shaking her head.

"Chile, he's your uncle. You know he does nothing simple," Denise chimed in.

"Nothing!" Alexis agreed.

"Absolutely nothing," said Peaches.

"I can only imagine what's in store for us all," Bobbie said with laughter.

They all followed me, giving me a hard time but still knew I had a wonderful time planned for them. Once checked into our rooms, the ladies found the itinerary on their bed. I heard Lashawn yell from across the hall, "Ah hell naw! I ain't doing this shit!"

"I'm on vacation. I just want to read and relax," Denise chimed.

"Come on, ladies. It's not that bad. Give Tyler a break. He put a lot of thought into planning this trip. Let's at least have a good time with it," Peaches argued.

"Peaches is right, you all. He put a lot of detail into this, even had the itinerary laminated," Bobbie burst into laughter.

"Once you ladies are done with all of your bickering, I will be downstairs ready for our first excursion. Look for the van that says Blue Horizon Travel," I said.

While I waited for them to come downstairs, Sinclair called, "Hey handsome. I just wanted to make sure you and the girls made it there safely. Where are you all staying?" he asked.

"At the Riu Santa Fe," I answered.

"Oh cool, enjoy yourselves. I have a friend that's staying there too, I think," he said.

"Nice, you should've come with your friend. We could've made some activities on the beach, you and I!" I said, laughing.

"Don't tempt me, young man. I'll fire up the company's jet and be there in a blink of an eye to have you eat those words. But I'm not going to hold you. I don't want your phone bill to be crazy. Miss you and have fun," he said.

"We haven't been here twenty minutes, and this dude has us going to ride horses on the beach," Alexis complained as she walked downstairs.

"I'll give him three out of the ten things he has listed for us," Lashawn chimed in.

"I'm heading over to make sure he's alright. Y'all hurt his feelings," Peaches said as she approached me. The rest of the girls were grumbling about the many excursions I had planned.

"Girl, don't let him play on your sympathy. He's spoiled, and trust me, his feelings aren't hurt," Bobbie assured her, and I giggled. She was right.

"Let's go, you all," Denise said, herding the crew over to where I stood waiting for the fun to begin.

"Ladies and gentleman, welcome to Los Cabos! I am Carlos and will be transporting you to Medano Beach for your horseback riding and parasailing excursions. I will pick you up after your lunch at Cachet Hotel," Carlos said with a winning smile.

"Carlos, are you from here?" Denise asked.

"Oh Lord, here comes Oprah Winfrey with her questions." Bobbie laughed.

"Si Senora, born and raised. Is this your first visit here?" Carlos asked.

"Yes, it is all of our first time, actually," Denise answered.

"Have you been given a copy of our itinerary, so you will know what time we have to be back at our hotel?" Lashawn laughed.

"Yes, ma'am. Blue Horizon Travel assigned me all of your transporting needs from your excursions to your nightlife," Carlos said confidently.

"Alright, Tyler, give me high five. Guess this may not be bad after all. You know I'm just giving you a hard time because you're still trying to run things like you did when we were children," Lashawn said.

"I've got you ladies covered. Now, let's go have some fun then lunch," I said.

After our parasailing and horseback riding along the beach, we sat out on the patio of the Cachet Hotel and ordered red snapper, grilled veggies, and cocktails.

"I'd like to make a toast," Peaches began.

"Glasses in the air, everybody," Bobbie commanded.

"To wonderful and new friendships and to Tyler's Angels," Peaches said.

"To Tyler's Angels," they all said in unison, clinking their glasses together.

"Thanks, ladies, for coming along with me. We are celebrating wonderful things today: new found freedom and new beginnings," I said. Once we were all done eating, Carlos was waiting on us to take us back to the Riu Santa Fe Hotel where we chilled until it was time for our 7 p.m. dinner reservations.

"Ladies, staying on schedule. I need you all dressed in your white and downstairs by 6:50 for our group pictures before our reservation at the El Farallon restaurant," I pleaded with the crew.

"We will be down in five minutes, Tyler. I'm keeping them on track," Alexis said.

"Thank you, AP. Kisses." I walked out of their room and headed downstairs.

* * *

After dinner, everyone rode to Mandala Los Cabos night club where Alexis made a connection with a handsome guy; they danced most of the night.

"How long are you visiting here? I'd like to have some time alone with you to show you around," he asked her.

"We are here for three more days. My friend has us on a tight schedule, but I can see if I can get away when they get their massages. I'll get out of it," Alexis said to her new friend.

"Do you smoke?" he asked.

"Only if you have some." Alexis laughed.

"Where are you staying? I'll come over and bring some. You sure you can get away for a bit?" he asked.

"If you bring some good fire, I'll make it happen. At the Riu Santa Fe," she said.

"What time is the massage tomorrow?" he asked.

"It is a ninety-minute massage scheduled at eleven on the beach," she responded.

"I see your girls keep eyeing you. I'm going to let you get back to them, and I'll see you in the morning, beautiful lady," he said kissing her silly on the dancefloor.

"Who was that fine hunk?" Peaches asked when she arrived back to the table.

"Just a little *situation* I'm going to kick it with while you all are getting your massages in the morning," Alexis answered.

"We are getting massages. How do you figure you'll get a pass?" Denise asked.

"I'm going to be on my cycle in the morning and will have heavy cramping going on. With Tyler being a massage therapist, he will understand the tenderness and discomfort I may be experiencing." Alexis laughed with a sly look on her face.

"Girl, you are too much!" Peaches laughed.

"Where's Tyler, Lashawn and Bobbie?" Alexis asked.

"Tyler saw Tamar Braxton over in the Chandelier Night Club recording a video, so they're over there having a cocktail, so he can see her," Denise explained.

"Not that I'm fond of her foolishness, but I guess it would be cool to actually watch the recording of a video. Let's go over there," Alexis suggested.

"Hey Tamar, girl!" a drunken Bobbie slurred.

"Now look Bobbie, you are not about to act a clown out here showing your ass. Pull it together," Lashawn ordered, pulling a staggering Bobbie onto the balcony of the club.

"Let me go!" Bobbie yelled as she snatched from Lashawn's grip.

"Okay, she has had enough. Let's catch a ride back to the resort so she can sober up," Denise said, stepping in.

~Los Cabos Day Two~

Denise, Bobbie, and Alexis were the first up and had gone down for breakfast. Me, Peaches and Lashawn slowly dragged our way out of the beds to join them.

"Mister, glad you and your late angels could join us," Bobbie said when we walked into the dining area.

"So, who is going first for the massages?" Denise asked.

"We are getting them at the same time on the beachside," I answered.

"Tyler, I'm going to pass. You all go get yours. Aunt Flo landed this morning, and I am cramping like a mofo," Alexis said.

"I totally understand that. Go lay down and rest, and hopefully, you will be better by the time we go for our ichthyotherapy appointment," I said.

"What in the hell! Tyler, I'm not doing that," Peaches screamed.

"Okay, clue me in. What's ichthyotherapy?" Bobbie asked.

"It's fish therapy. You place your feet in water with toothless carp that nibble away dead, calloused skin from the feet," Lashawn answered.

"I will pass on that, too," Bobbie said.

"I am going, Tyler," Lashawn said.

"We can discuss this later. We have less than seven minutes to make it down by the beach for our massages," I said.

"See you all later. I'm going to lay down. Enjoy your massage," Alexis said.

* * *

While everyone else was at the beach, Alexis was awaiting her *situation* to show up.

"Good morning, sexy mama. Your Prince is here," he said when he arrived.

"Come on in. The coast is clear. Did you bring some smoke?" Alexis asked.

"Yes, I did, Ma. Where do you want to smoke it?" he asked.

"On the balcony?" she shrugged her shoulders.

"This is some potent stuff. It's so good you're going to want me to eat on that pretty puss of yours," he warned.

"Well, if you got some good tongue action, I just might let you do that," she teased.

"Why don't I go out on the balcony and fire it up while you put on something less fitting, no panties, and meet me out here?" he asked.

"You're talking my kind of language!" Alexis said.

When she walked onto the balcony, Prince had the lounger flat as he laid back. "Ma, come sit on my face and puff on this shit." He handed her the blunt, and she started puffing.

"I don't know which is better, your tongue action or this fire ass shit. You can really eat some pussy!" she moaned.

* * *

I wanted our next to the last night to be perfect, so I had Piece of Cake ship a white chocolate cake to the hotel to celebrate my love for these beautiful women. I ordered their entrees and cocktails and had them brought to the private beach area off from our room where our guest services agent, Luciana, had chairs, a bonfire, and a small table with the cake, plates, forks, napkins, and a cutting knife all sitting on it.

"Dude, you are so extra. You never cease to amaze us. You do it big or not at all right?" Peaches asked.

"You don't know the half of it, Peaches," Bobbie said as she cut the cake. She passed everyone a plate around as they ate and moaned about how delicious it was.

Denise started playing music, and we were all dancing, lightly kicking sand, and having the time of our lives like grade school kids. We line danced to the "Wobble." Then, she played the "Biker Shuffle;" only she and I could do that. Then, Alexis grabbed the iPod.

"We don't know what that shit is. Let's have something we all know," she said and played the "Electric Slide."

As the song ended, I grabbed the iPod and found "Candlelight and You." I waited until they calmed down; I knew once the song started playing Lashawn would jump into her role and be ready to sing Keith Washington's verse as I led Chante' Moore's verse. As the song played, I went into character, and Lashawn yelled, "Ah shit, here's our song!"

She stood up and made her way to me. She started rocking and using her fork for her microphone. Midway through the song, Eli FaceTime'd my phone, but I didn't feel the vibration of the call. We were so into the song, and we were in our zone. Eli had something going on the other end that he needed to share with me right then, so he FaceTime'd Bobbie.

"Bobbie, where is Tyler? I'm trying to reach him," Eli asked her.

"Since this is next to the last night here, we are spending it on the beach by a bonfire and Tyler and Lashawn are over there singing their song," Bobbie said.

"Uh oh, 'Candlelight and You?'" he asked.

"Yes." She turned the phone around so he could watch everyone having a great time singing and bobbing their heads to the song. Eli was trying to get Bobbie's attention.

"Bobbie, Bobbie can you hear me?" he asked to have her turn the screen back around because he wanted to show her something.

As they were finishing up the chorus to the song, we all heard the sound of a violin playing Floetry's "Say Yes" playing. There were flames following the music and the sight of white fabric flowing approaching us.

Eli asked, "Bobbie, what is going on?"

"I don't know. We are trying to make out what or who this is coming up on us with flames and music," she whispered.

"Sinclair?" Peaches yelled.

"Peaches?" Sinclair sighed.

"Why are you here?" she asked.

I stood there wondering how they knew one another and what he was doing on our trip with this big production.

"Bobbie, turn the phone around, so I can see you. I want to tell you something. When you all return from Cabo, I'm going to give Tyler this ring," Eli said. He opened the David Yurman box and showed Bobbie a beautiful three-row band ring with Sapphire.

"Let me turn the phone around so you can do it now in front of everyone," Bobbie suggested.

Just as she turned the phone around to let him propose to me, Sinclair kneeled in front of me and said, "Babe, inside this manila envelope I have your final divorce decree you wanted from Isabella. Now that you no longer have to worry about being married to her..." Sinclair reached into his pocket and pulled out a Cartier box and asked, "Will you marry me?"

Have you read the beginning of Tyler's story?

HE WAS MY HUSBAND TOO...

ABOUT THE AUTHOR

Anthony K. Robinson, the youngest of eight children, was born to the late Gradie Mae and the late Laton Robinson in Alexander City, Alabama, on June 4, 1969. Anthony lost his father, who was shot, just shortly after his birth. His late grandmother Mary Etta (Big Mama) and sister Martha Nell were very vocal and supportive in assisting his mother with his upbringing.

Anthony was raised in a middle-class household. In school, he was sometimes ridiculed and judged for his mannerism and high-pitched voice, by his peers and sometimes his brothers. However, that didn't discourage him. It actually made him act out and embrace who he was even more. Under the direction of his grandmother, he found Christ at an early age. He, along with his niece and nephew, went to church every Sunday morning, Sunday evening, and every Wednesday.

Upon not passing the enlistment exam for the Air Force in 1987, Anthony moved to Birmingham to pursue an Associates Degree in Computer Programming. With one semester remaining until graduation, Anthony still felt something was missing in his life. He called his mother, told her how unhappy he was, and then he moved home to go to cosmetology school. He put himself through cosmetology school by seeing clients from dusk to dawn every Saturday. In Alabama, he worked in a salon, thenceforth decided to relocate and make Atlanta his home. Presently, he has been a Cosmetologist, Massage Therapist, Esthetician and Educator for a combined 28 years.